Beyond the Hate

D. E. Haggerty

Also by D.E. Haggerty

Before It Was Love
After The Vows
While We Waited
All Along
How to Date a Rockstar
How to Love a Rockstar
How to Fall For a Rockstar
How to Be a Rockstar's Girlfriend
How to Catch a Rockstar
My Forever Love
Forever For You
Just For Forever
Stay For Forever
Only Forever
Meet Disaster
Meet Not
Meet Dare
Meet Hate
Bragg's Truth
Bragg's Love

Perfect Bragg
Bragg's Match
Bragg's Christmas
A Hero for Hailey
A Protector for Phoebe
A Soldier for Suzie
A Fox for Faith
A Christmas for Chrissie
A Valentine for Valerie
A Love for Lexi
About Face
At Arm's Length
Hands Off
Knee Deep
Molly's Misadventures

Chapter 1

Paisley – a woman who has no intention of being dragged into her friends' matchmaking games

PAISLEY

"This is utterly ridiculous. I'm not doing it."

"Please, please, please, please," Chloe begs as she jumps up and down.

"I'm not the singer of the group."

I nod to Maya who holds up her hands. "I'm not allowed to sing. Mermaid Karaoke is for single ladies."

I hate to repeat myself but, "Mermaid Karaoke is ridiculous."

Women dressed up as mermaids – complete with seashell bras – and singing on a stage to attract men is absurd.

"It's a tradition," Sophia says.

I purse my lips since she is unfortunately correct. Smuggler's Hideaway – the island on which we live – is fond of hosting quirky and mystical based events to attract tourists. Based on how crowded the *Bootlegger* bar is, it's working.

"Come on," Nova cajoles. "You're the only single member of our group left."

Thanks for the reminder. Merely a year ago at this very Mermaid Karaoke festival, all five of us were single.

But then Sophia got together with her brother's best friend, the boy she's been in love with forever. Chloe married her neighbor to save his daughter and fell in love. Nova got pregnant with the resort owner's baby and now they're engaged. And, finally, Maya is at long last engaged to the man she's been obsessed with since high school.

A wave of jealousy punches me in the stomach, but I ignore it. I'm happy for Maya. I truly am. It's not her fault the boy I liked in high school is a Grade A asshole.

"None of you sang Mermaid Karaoke when you were single. In fact, I distinctly remember us avoiding *Bootlegger* and drinking at the *Rumrunner* bar instead."

Maya holds up her hand. "I sang Mermaid Karaoke."

"And you were marvelous."

I'm not just saying this to give my shy friend a confidence boost. She really was marvelous. Maya can sing. Which is why Chloe dared her to join the choir in high school. Maya was afraid to join even though she loves singing. But no one can resist a dare from Chloe. She won't let you.

Nova smiles as she motions to the stage. "Why don't you go be marvelous?"

I snort. "Because the sound of my singing reminds Chloe of fingernails on a chalkboard."

Chloe cringes. "I didn't say the sound was bad."

I hold up my hand. "There's no reason to backpedal. I'm self aware. I know I can't sing."

Sophia leans close to whisper in Chloe's ear. "Too bad she isn't self aware about how much she wants to get into Eli's pants."

Eli. It always comes back to Eli with this group. This is the problem with having friends you've known since you were in diapers. They know all about your past – including secret crushes you'd rather everyone forgot about.

Although, they don't know my biggest secret. I never did tell them why Eli moved from the 'crush' column to the 'I want nothing to do with him' column in high school. And I never will. I prefer to avoid humiliation when I can. Thus, my refusal to sing Mermaid Karaoke.

Fortunately for me, I have an ace up my sleeve.

"You do know mermaids aren't real."

Chloe gasps and Nova clutches her chest while Maya glares at me. The residents of Smuggler's Hideaway are big believers in mermaids. There's even a legend about a mermaid who threw herself off of the cliffs near *Mermaid Mystical Gardens* when her lover drowned.

The legends are good for tourism. They're also a fallacy.

And completely unnecessary to draw tourists to the island. There are enough true stories about smugglers and their use of the island to hide their loot during Prohibition. There are even 'secret' underground passages under city hall visitors can tour.

Sophia sighs. "I thought we were past this when you agreed to name the Saison beer Mystic Mermaid Saison."

"I agreed because you convinced me the name would be good for marketing."

Sophia is the marketing manager of the brewery the five of us own, *Five Fathoms Brewing.* Since marketing is not my area of expertise – my expertise is limited to the brewing of beer – I followed her advice with regard to the name of our latest Saison beer.

"Based on sales, the idea was great," Maya says.

Maya is the financial manager for the brewery. Sales and numbers I understand. They are fact based after all.

"Customers are loving it," Chloe adds. "I ran out of stock on the first night at the bar."

In addition to brewing beer, *Five Fathoms* also has a bar and restaurant. Chloe manages them.

"And it's easy to sell to our clients," Nova says.

Everything is easy to sell for Nova. The woman smiles and people rush to do her bidding. Which is good for *Five Fathoms* since she's our sales manager.

Sophia glares at me. I lift my eyebrows. "What?"

"You changed the subject to beer."

"You're the one who brought up our Saison beer."

"If you don't go up there and sing, I'm going to steal moonshine from those women." Chloe points to a table of women dressed as mermaids. Guessing by the way they're swaying to the music, they've had enough moonshine.

I snort. "You've been eyeing their table for five minutes. You're going to steal their moonshine anyway."

She huffs. "Could you be less observant for five minutes?"

Not really. I've tried to be less observant. To not notice everything happening around me. To not remember every conversation we have. To bite my tongue before I note another fact no one cares about.

It didn't work so I leaned into it instead. And Paisley the Perpetual Know It All was born.

My stomach sours. I sincerely hate the nickname everyone in high school loved to taunt me with. I especially hate the boy who coined the phrase.

And there I go thinking about Eli again.

I simply can't eradicate him from my thoughts. The cute boy from high school with jet black hair and bright blue eyes has become a handsome man with a deep, gravelly voice I long to hear the sound of. And then there are those muscles. Why does a billionaire have a need for strong biceps and wide shoulders?

He should—

I cut those thoughts off. I am usually in perfect control of my thoughts. But not when it comes to *him*.

I blame his return to the island. I was fine when he was off living his billionaire life somewhere else. But he moved back to Smuggler's Hideaway a few months ago and now my mind conjures him at the oddest of times. It's beyond annoying.

There is one surefire way to get my mind and everyone else's off of Eli. I can challenge Chloe.

"I dare you to jump on this table, run across the room to the bar without touching the floor and without getting caught by Sloane."

"Or any of the security," Sophia adds.

Chloe rubs her hands together. "I got this."

"I thought you weren't the wild child anymore," Nova says.

Chloe has a bit of a reputation for being wild. Although, really, no one in this friend group can point fingers. We've all gotten into our fair share of trouble. None of which was instigated by me. Naturally.

Chloe winks at Nova. "I'm not a child." She kicks off her shoes before jumping onto the table.

"Maybe we should add she's not allowed to waste alcohol," Maya mutters as she rushes to save our beers before Chloe knocks them off of our table.

"Don't you worry. I don't abuse alcohol. Are we timing this?"

Sophia jiggles her phone. "Got it."

"Don't use your phone," Nova says. "We'll need it to contact your brother, Weston, when Chloe's detained."

Chloe snorts. "Weston's not the only cop on this island. My husband's one, too. I'm not getting arrested."

Maya sighs. "She truly believes she won't get arrested because Lucas is a police officer."

For good reason. Lucas would never allow her to be arrested. Even if she deserves it. Which she often does in my opinion.

"Ten, nine, eight," Sophia counts down.

Others in the bar notice Chloe on the table and Sophia counting down and join in. They have no idea what's happening but smugglers are troublemakers down to their bones. If they notice shenanigans, they won't snitch. They'll sooner join in. And let chaos reign.

"Five, four, three, two, one. GO!"

Chloe jumps to the next table and people scramble to remove their drinks before they fall. "Bar." She motions in the direction of the bar and people hurry out of her way.

The mermaid stops singing and the music changes to *Bad Boys*. Chloe throws her hands up in the air and sings along. I cringe. There's a reason no one besides Maya ever sang karaoke.

The bartender climbs onto the bar. She crosses her arms and glares at Chloe. Uh oh. Sloane's pissed.

I cough to hide my grin. I knew there was no way Sloane wouldn't stop Chloe. The bartender has had her eye on us since we showed up at the bar. And she wasn't subtle about it either. Nope. She tapped her eyes and shouted, "I'm watching you!" across the bar.

Chloe skids to a halt on the table in front of Sloane.

"It's as if you want me to ban you from my bar," Sloane says.

"You ban us from the bar *Five Fathoms* won't supply you beer anymore."

"You willing to take the risk?" Sloane challenges.

The door bangs open and Lucas and Weston stride inside. They must be on duty since they're in uniform. Chloe's husband, Lucas, takes in the scene and drops his chin to his chest with a sigh.

Weston slaps him on the back. "You owe me twenty bucks."

Three men rush into the bar behind Lucas and Weston. Maya, Nova, and Sophia hurry across the bar to their partners – Caleb, Hudson, and Flynn. And I'm left behind.

I'm always left behind. The sole woman in the group who doesn't have a man. And never will. Been there. Done that. Have the scars on my heart to prove it.

Chapter 2

Eli – a billionaire who'd rather be on an island with his shit stirring brothers than in a board room with his shit stirring colleagues

ELI

"Are you listening to me?"

I draw a hand down my face. "Can you repeat the last part?"

Jeremy barks out a laugh. "Dude, I have never seen you this distracted. Not even when you came back to college from Thanksgiving break with a case of poison ivy. You sat for your finals with a cold compress on your forehead."

"Don't remind me." Having five younger brothers who are the definition of shit stirrers is a damn trial.

He waggles his eyebrows. "Is it a woman?"

I shake my head even as a vision of Paisley pops into my mind. Paisley and her long auburn hair with out of control curls. Her hazel eyes always narrowing and flashing with anger whenever she looks at me. The freckles across her nose I want to count with my tongue.

Does she have freckles anywhere else on her body? How I'd love to strip her bare to find out. My cock twitches. It's on board with the idea.

"Not a woman," I lie.

"Which is why your eyes went all dreamy and you zoned out for a minute."

I glare at him. "My eyes didn't go dreamy."

He holds up his hands. "At least tell me it isn't Miranda who you're dreaming about."

I scowl. "Not Miranda."

He drags the back of his hand across his forehead in an exaggerated gesture of relief. "Phew."

I roll my eyes. "She's not too bad."

He chuckles. "Your secretary has been through the entire board of directors. She came on to each and every one of them – man and woman alike. You're the only one who can put up with her since you're hardly here anymore."

I frown. Is he upset I don't live in California any longer? "You agreed I could move back to Smuggler's Hideaway and work remotely."

There's no need for me to be at the headquarters of *Apparoo* anymore. In the beginning, when Jeremy had the idea for his app and it was all hands on deck to develop the software and build the business, things were different. But the company is pretty steady now.

I can do most of my work as Chief Financial Officer from Smuggler's Hideaway. Besides being present for meetings every now and again, there's no reason for me to be physically present at the headquarters.

"I was merely pointing out a fact."

I study him. He appears serious. But my former college roommate is a master bullshitter. In college, he'd invent the most outlandish reasons why his assignment was late and the professors would buy it – hook, line, and sinker. I'm still surprised he managed to graduate at all – let alone in four years.

"I don't want my move to come between us."

"I get it. You want to be near your family. And since *Buccaneer's Whiskey & Distillery* is making waves in the industry, they need you there to guide them through the transition from local distillery to worldwide domination."

"I never mentioned anything about worldwide domination."

"But you're Eli Raider. You don't know how to not dominate the world." He throws his arms wide open. "Look at what you've accomplished here."

"I think you're forgetting about how you're some genius coder who turns the most outrageous idea for an app into a million dollar line of revenue."

He pats himself on the back. "It's true. I am a genius."

"And modest, too."

Jeremy stands. "Come on. It's time for the meeting."

As soon as I step out of my office, Miranda jumps out of her chair. "Mr. Raider. Do you need my assistance?"

I barely stop myself from rolling my eyes at how she purrs her question. I pat my laptop. "I'm good."

She isn't deterred. She follows us to the meeting room. "What about a coffee?"

I indicate the table where several carafes of coffee and tea are set out.

Jeremy stops her before she can enter the room. "We're good, Miranda. Go back to your desk."

She licks her lips as she stares up at him. After a few moments of him staring down at her, she huffs and whirls around before stomping back to her desk.

Jeremy chuckles as he sits at the table. "You have to give her credit. She's persistent."

I shrug. I have no interest in my secretary. She's not the one who heats my blood. "She does her job well."

"Do you have the presentation ready?"

I narrow my eyes at him. "I'm not the one who thinks a deadline is a suggestion."

"People get way too worked up about deadlines."

"Sometimes it's hard to believe you're a billionaire."

"Hey!" He points a finger at me. "You are, too."

"Because I invested in your app."

When Jeremy asked for seed money to launch his app company while we were still in college, I offered him the money I'd saved up for the next semester's tuition. I figured I'd never see the money again and would have to take out a loan for tuition.

Instead, the app had more than one thousand downloads on the first day. And from there, things went crazy.

"Don't sell yourself short. You worked just as hard as I did those first few years out of college."

Between being the CFO for *Apparoo* and the CEO of *Buccaneer's Whiskey,* I still work my ass off. But now, instead of couch surfing to save money, I have a luxurious apartment here in California and my dream house on Smuggler's Hideaway.

Life is good. If a bit lonely. Thoughts of Paisley flash into my mind again but I force them out. A senior management meeting is not the time or place to think about the woman who hates my guts.

I wake up my laptop and connect it to the screen. I open my presentation and *Help me!* screeches from the speakers.

"What the hell?" I press escape to get out of the presentation but nothing happens.

Jeremy bursts into laughter. "Look."

On the big screen, a man labelled Eli is being chased by a shark labeled Miranda. The theme song of *Jaws* plays in the background while the cartoon Eli screams for help.

"It's a good thing the other managers haven't arrived yet," Jeremy manages to say between his barks of laughter.

I glare at him.

He holds up his hands. "It's not me who pranked the IT team."

I grit my teeth. "It was an accident."

"An accident? Their coffee machine broke and you were doused in coffee. You could have at least covered your tracks."

I throw my arms in the air. "For the last time. I didn't break the machine. I was trying to fix it."

He pats my shoulder. "Maybe you should stick to numbers instead of actual machinery."

I growl at him. "Says the man who doesn't know how a toilet plunger works."

"You're the one who wanted to go out for Mexican food."

"You could have told me you were allergic to Chipotle peppers."

"I didn't know."

I narrow my eyes on him. "You'd never eaten Mexican food before in your life?"

"We've been over this. It's not my fault I never ordered extra spicy before."

The door opens and the senior management team begins to file in. I check my watch. They're late. All of them are late. Which is highly unusual.

"Is it over?" Jennifer, the human resources manager, asks.

I study the team and notice everyone is averting their eyes. Were they warned about the prank? "Is what over?"

She motions to my laptop. "Whatever juvenile prank happened I do not want to know about it."

Jennifer tries to keep everyone in line and ensure there is no bullying or mistreatment of employees. Considering we're a company of people who've mostly known each other since college and believe pranking is the highest form of affection there is, she's often forced to look the other way.

I sigh. "I can't wait to get back home."

"What's on this island you can't stay away from?" Jeremy asks. "Maybe we should visit for a company retreat."

"No!"

"Testy. It's probably because the woman who rejected him is there."

Paisley never rejected me. I've never had the chance to ask her out considering she runs the other way whenever I'm around. Hell, she even hid behind a bar once.

The woman does not like me. I wish I could say the feeling is mutual.

"Are we going to conduct this meeting or not?" I make a show of checking my watch. "I have a plane to catch."

"You own the jet. I think they'll wait for you to arrive."

"I bet we could fit all of the senior management team in his jet," Chuck, the operations manager, says. "I can be packed in five minutes."

I growl at him. "You're not coming to Smuggler's Hideaway with me."

The island is my sanctuary. No one treats me like a billionaire there. To them, I'm Eli. The oldest son of Jessica. The oldest brother of Jaxon, Rhett, Kai, Miles, and Zane.

No one kowtows to me because of my money on the island. They don't care. One person in particular who I want to care, doesn't give a shit about me.

And there I go thinking about Paisley again. I need to figure out a way to stop obsessing over her.

Chapter 3

"Next time. Call someone else." ~ Paisley

PAISLEY

I finish mixing the ingredients together and swirl them around in the beaker. This is my favorite part about being a brewer – coming up with new flavors. As a microbrewery, *Five Fathoms* has the freedom to create fun and unique beers national brewers can't take a chance on.

My phone rings and I check the time. It's ten a.m. This is my favorite time to concentrate on work. Which is why my phone is on *Do Not Disturb*. Even my girlfriends don't bother me at this time. There must be some kind of emergency.

"Paisley!" Parker shouts when I answer the phone.

I frown. Why is the owner of *Pirate's Pastries* contacting me? Don't get me wrong. Parker and I are friends. She was a class behind me in school but on an island the size of Smuggler's Hideaway one year doesn't make a difference.

"What's wrong?"

"I have a problem."

"What kind of problem?"

"I need you. Can you come to the bakery?"

I stand with a sigh. "Of course. I'll be there in five minutes."

"Come quick," she insists and hangs up. She still hasn't explained what the problem is.

I hang my lab coat on the hook behind the door in my lab. "I'm heading out," I tell my assistant, Blossom.

"Where are you going? When will you return?"

"I have no idea, but I will inform you when I know more."

"Is this an owners of the brewery get together?"

I shrug since I don't know the answer to her question. Granted, Parker rang me and not one of my friends, but my friends are troublemakers who know I won't answer the phone in the morning when I'm in the lab.

I don't bother driving or biking to the bakery. It's a three-minute walk from *Five Fathoms* to *Pirates Pastries.* The brewery is located on the outskirts of Smuggler's Rest, which is the largest town on the island of Smuggler's Hideaway.

The other two towns, Pirate's Perch and Rogue's Landing, are more hamlets than actual towns. All of the necessary amenities are in Smuggler's Rest.

I arrive at the bakery but when I try the door, it's locked. I knock. "Hello! Parker?"

She rushes to the door. "Back door!"

This better not be some kind of prank. I try to recall if I've in some way incurred Parker's wrath but besides buying out all of her Shipwreck cookies for Maya and Caleb's housewarming celebration, I haven't seen her much.

The back door flies open as I round the corner. "Get in here. Quick!"

"What is happening? If this is some prank, can we postpone until after working hours?"

"No prank. I have a situation." She snatches my hand and drags me through the kitchen to the bakery.

"What is—" The question dies in my mouth when I notice the man inside the bakery. Eli Raider. My archnemesis.

Archnemesis you want to ride like a cowboy, a voice in the back of my mind says but I ignore it. As I usually do. It's the voice responsible for getting me into trouble more than once in the past.

I yank my hand away from Parker. "This isn't funny."

"I know." She wrings her hands. "He's scaring off customers."

I frown. "Eli's scaring off customers?"

"What?" Her brow wrinkles. "Eli? No." She points to the ground. "Him."

I search the floor but all I see are tiles and some cookie crumbs. There's nothing untoward.

Eli clears his throat. "I think he's hiding underneath the display case."

"Who is hiding beneath the display case?"

I don't wait for them to answer before kneeling next to the case and peaking underneath. I notice motion out of the corner of my eye but whatever it is, is too fast for me to make out.

"He's out!" Eli screams and climbs onto a table.

I stand and brush my hands off of my jeans. "Who's out?"

He gestures to the corner. "That thing!"

I scan the corner, but I don't see anything. "Have you been putting hallucinogens in your muffins again?" I ask Parker.

"One time. One time I put some mushrooms in a batch of Pirate's Plunder Muffins. And you totally deserved it."

I hold up my hands. "I wasn't the one who stole your clothes."

"Chloe and Sophia might have been the ones to steal my clothes but you didn't help when I came out of the ocean completely naked."

I roll my eyes. "It's not my fault you enjoy skinny dipping."

"But you—"

"Ladies!" Eli shouts. "Can you two reminisce about the past at another time? Maybe when there isn't a rodent running around the bakery trying to kill me."

"Rodent? What rodent?" I ask.

"Viking may have accidentally found his way into the bakery," Parker answers.

"Viking's in the bakery?" I ask.

Viking is the otter mascot for Smuggler's Rest. Each town on the island has a live mascot. Rogue's Landing has a raccoon and Pirate's Perch has a parrot. During the summer, townspeople try to steal the mascots from the other towns. Which is why the locations of the mascots are closely guarded secrets.

Parker bites her lip. "Y-y-es."

"And he's trying to kill me!" Eli shouts.

He's standing on the table now. In a three-piece suit and tie. I glance down at my outfit. I'm wearing faded jeans and a worn t-shirt with the words *I stop for seals* on it.

"Otters aren't rodents. They're part of the Mustelidae family, which is a family of carnivorous mammals. The family includes skunks, weasels, wolverines, and badgers."

"Can you sprout random, useless facts at another time? Maybe when I'm not being attacked by an animal?"

I snort to hide how much his words hurt. He didn't call me Paisley the Perpetual Know It All but he might as well have. "Viking is nowhere near you. Besides, otters rarely attack humans. And Viking is domesticated."

"Domesticated my ass! He bit my foot." He lifts up his leather shoe which probably cost more than the entire bakery.

"Are you seriously complaining about a scuff on your shoe? Did you forget you're a smuggler?"

His eyes narrow on me. Try as I might, I can't help but notice how piercing those blue eyes are. I want to drown in them while he caresses my body. I imagine his hands are smooth and callus free.

No. No. No. I don't want any of those things. Eli Raider is a Class A jerk. And I've had my fill of jerks. You can say what you want about me but I do learn from my mistakes.

"I'm not an idiot. I know otters can carry rabies."

I place my hands on my hips and glare at Eli. "Did Viking actually puncture your skin or did he bump your leg because he wanted you to give him a treat?"

Eli scowls. "A treat? I'm in a bakery. There shouldn't be an otter running around."

My mood skyrockets from mildly irritated to red hot anger in a millisecond. Parker is having a hard enough time keeping her bakery afloat. If this jerk goes around claiming he got bit by an otter in *Pirates Pastries,* she'll be out of business in no time. Not on my watch.

I stomp toward him. "This isn't some California hippie bakery. This is Smuggler's Hideaway. Don't you dare spread rumors about the hygiene in *Pirates Pastries.* My access to chemistry supplies has multiplied since you last lived on the island."

His nostrils flare but when he opens his mouth to speak, I wag my finger at him.

"Do you understand what I'm saying?"

In other words, do I need to remind him about the time his locker exploded? He knows it was me who pranked him in high school since I took full credit. I wanted him to know it was me. Trust me. He deserved it after what he did.

He grits his teeth. "Can you please catch the animal? I would like to leave."

I debate my answer. Watching Eli panic is fun, but, on the other hand, I don't want to be in the same room as him.

"I can."

I snatch a couple of Blackbeard's revenge cookies from the display case and settle in the corner on the floor of the bakery. "Viking, I have your favorite," I sing.

I continue to sing his name until the otter peaks out from underneath the display case. I coo at him. "Hey, sweetie. How have you been?"

I'll never admit it out loud, but I was Viking's secret keeper for a year. Since he mostly preferred to be left alone and I'm a bit of a workaholic, the relationship worked.

Except for when I brought home cookies from the bakery. The little sneak would steal every single one of them if I didn't lock them away.

It isn't long before Viking sprints across the floor to steal the cookie from me. He sits in front of me and devours it while watching me. I swear he's smirking at me.

"You need to return to your cage before Parker gets into trouble."

He chirps to indicate his disapproval.

"Sorry, sweetie. Rules are rules."

Parker tiptoes toward me with his cage. She sets it down behind him as quietly as she can but of course, Viking hears. He hisses at her.

"Stop it, Viking," I order and hand him another cookie.

While he's eating, I pick him up and place him in the cage. If he could roll his eyes at me, he would.

"Thank you," Parker whispers as she tiptoes away with him.

I stand and nearly rear back when I come face to face with Eli. I didn't realize he'd left the safety of his table.

"Wow. You're good with him."

I frown at him. "You don't have to sound surprised."

He holds up his hands. "It was merely a comment."

"Whatever." I wipe the dirt from my jeans. "I need to return to the brewery."

I walk away without a backward glance. I refuse to obsess about Eli since he's returned to the island. He's not worth any mental energy I expend on him.

I will never experience those piercing blue eyes spark with passion. It's better this way.

Chapter 4

"Sometimes I wish I was an only child." ~ Eli

ELI

I smile as I enter *Buccaneer's Whiskey & Distillery.* This is my dream. Maybe not the distillery itself but owning a business with my five brothers? It's everything I wished for after Dad left us.

I bite back the temptation to growl. Dad is such an asshole for abandoning Mom to bring up six kids on her own. I will never forgive him for what he did. And I definitely won't forgive him for showing up at my door in California begging for money. Acting as if he deserved it.

"Uh oh," my assistant, Dakota, mutters as I enter the offices of the distillery. "Someone's grumpy today."

"I'm not grumpy."

"And you're not a big fat liar either."

"I wouldn't say fat."

She giggles. "Nope. Not an ounce of fat on you, is there?"

If Miranda said those words, I'd worry she was coming onto me. But with Dakota, I have no such worries. I'm not the brother she's interested in.

"Are any of my brothers in yet?"

Her gaze darts to Rhett's office. "Mr. High and Mighty is in his office and Jaxon is in the lab. Miles, Zane, and Kai aren't in yet."

I'm not surprised. Miles prefers to spend his days on a surfboard. Kai is never on time. And Zane does whatever Zane wants.

I check my watch. We have a meeting scheduled in thirty minutes. "Can you call them? Get them here on time for the meeting?"

"You should listen to me and schedule the meeting an hour before the time you actually want to meet."

"Or my brothers could learn some discipline."

She laughs. "Sure. That'll happen."

I hate how right she is. I stepped in when Dad left to help Mom raise my brothers but with six of us kids, Mom working two jobs, and working three jobs myself, there simply weren't enough hours in the day to deal with my shit stirring brothers.

"I'll be in my office if you need me."

She salutes me before returning her attention to her computer. She's a damn good assistant. I sincerely hope my brother doesn't screw things up with her and cause her to quit. Maybe I should remind him to keep his hands off of her.

I spend the next half hour preparing for our meeting and dodging phone calls. My brothers and I don't meet often.

When we do, it's important. I fear today's meeting is going to be a clash. And when my brothers clash? Watch out.

Dakota knocks on my door. "Everyone's here."

"You don't need to notify him. He can tell time," Rhett grumbles from behind her.

I stand and button my suit jacket. "Thanks, Dakota. You're an angel."

Rhett growls and Dakota rolls her eyes. "Mr. High and Mighty isn't in the meeting room yet."

I cough to hide my amusement at my brother's irritation with my assistant. I really do need to remember to tell him to keep his hands to himself. I won't lose a good assistant because my brother is horny.

I join Rhett in the hallway and together we walk to the meeting room. When we enter, I frown when I notice Kai is missing. I don't know why I expected my youngest brother to be on time. He never is.

I settle in a chair next to Miles. I sniff. "Why do I smell seawater?"

He shakes his head and water droplets fly onto the table and my suit jacket.

My nostrils flare in irritation as I wipe the water off of me, but I inhale a deep breath before I lash out at him. "Did you go surfing this morning?"

"Bro, I surf every morning."

"I told you today's meeting is important. You couldn't have at least changed into dry clothes?"

"Dakota gave me a towel to sit on. I won't ruin your precious chairs."

"I don't care about the chairs. I care about this business."

"Bro, you're a billionaire. What does it matter?"

I grit my teeth. He makes it sound like being a billionaire is no big deal. Like I didn't exist on cheap Ramen noodles and three hours of sleep for a decade.

Worse yet? He's trashing *Buccaneer's Whiskey & Distillery.*

"Because this is *our* business. The Raider brothers' business. It's our legacy."

His nose wrinkles. "It's not the legacy I want."

All my rancor evaporates at his words. Miles' dream was to be a professional surfer. And he was good enough to make it as a pro, but after he tore his rotator cuff at a competition in Hawaii, his dreams disappeared in a puff of smoke. He can still surf, but his range of motion is too limited for a professional.

"Sorry, bro."

He scowls at me. "I don't need your pity."

"Good because you're not getting any pity from me. Next time you show up at a meeting in wet surf clothes, I'll make you stand in the corner."

"With a dunce cap," Zane adds. "Can we get him a little stool, too? And make him face the corner?"

"I'll show you a dunce cap," Miles mutters before flying over the table at Zane.

Rhett maneuvers his way in between the two and pulls them apart. "Enough," he grumbles.

"You're no fun," Zane claims as he returns to his seat.

"Fuddy duddy," Miles adds.

"Can we begin this meeting now?" Jaxon asks.

"What's your rush?" Zane asks.

Jaxon purses his lips. "Do you not understand what this meeting is about? Regardless of the outcome, my workload is going to quadruple."

Miles rolls his eyes. "Nerd."

"Hey!" I holler. "No name calling."

"It's not name calling when it's the truth. Jaxon is a nerd." Miles motions to his brother. "Check him out. Glasses, shirt buttoned to his neck. I'm surprised he doesn't have a pocket protector."

"Pocket protectors are for geeks. Not nerds," Zane says.

"Bro," Miles mutters, and they high-five each other.

The door to the meeting room opens and Kai appears. Finally. We can get this meeting started before a brawl breaks out. Jaxon may be a nerd but he's a dirty fighter. All of my brothers are. Doc Allens, at the hospital, can attest to how dirty.

"Watch out, Eli. Viking is coming to get you." Kai throws a stuffed animal into the room before bursting into laughter.

I drop my head into my hands. I should have known everyone would find out about what happened at the bakery. The smugglers' grapevine is incredibly effective. And Paisley probably couldn't wait to share my fear of Viking the otter with the rest of the island's inhabitants.

"What's this about?" Jaxon asks as he picks up the stuffed otter.

"Eli's afraid of otters," Kai says.

"I heard he screamed like a little girl when he saw Viking," Miles adds.

"Nope." Zane shakes his head. "He peed his pants."

I growl. "I did not pee my pants and I didn't scream like a little girl."

"But he did jump onto a table and make a woman save him," Kai says.

"Not any woman. Paisley." Miles waggles his eyebrows.

"Isn't Paisley the girl you had a crush on in high school?" Rhett asks.

I glare at him. "I didn't have a crush on her."

"Then, why did you moan her name when you jacked off?" Jaxon asks.

"If you don't want a stuffed otter shoved down your throat, you'll shut the fuck up."

Miles, Zane, and Kai dissolve into laughter. Miles bends over and grabs his stomach. Zane pounds a palm on the table. And Kai dances around the room with the stuffed toy.

"Are we going to discuss business today?" I ask the room.

"I hope we are," Jaxon says. "I need to make preparations either way."

Miles' laughter cuts off. "Either way? What are you referring to?"

Jaxon's brow wrinkles. "Didn't you read Eli's memo?" Miles snorts and Jaxon sighs. "Of course not. Why did I bother asking?"

"What did it say?" Miles asks.

"We need to decide between expanding our whiskey and gin distilling facilities or adding rum to our list of products," I explain.

"Bro, I said from the beginning. We need rum. Bootleggers loved rum," Zane says.

"Adding rum to our list of products would require us to buy additional equipment as well as Jaxon learning a new method of distilling."

Kai rolls his eyes. "Jaxon is smarter than the rest of us combined. He can probably sleep on a book about rum production and know more than the experts the next morning."

"There's also the need for increased cleaning protocols as the molasses can cause sticky residue in the equipment," Rhett adds. "And this will cut into the profit margin."

"It's all about the money with him," Zane whisper-shouts to Kai.

"What does moneybags want to do?" Miles asks and everyone's attention returns to me.

"It's not as if the rest of you are destitute," I mutter.

"Because of you," Rhett says.

"Come on." Miles elbows me. "What do you want to do? You know we'll agree with your decision."

Kai raises his hand. "I won't. I want rum."

"Really?" I lift an eyebrow. "Can you even stand the smell of rum?"

His hand falls. "If it's not too close."

"Oh, man." Zane feigns a shiver. "I forgot about the time he drank a bottle of Malibu rum. His pores reeked of coconut for weeks."

"Too bad his puke didn't smell of coconut since he threw up every-freaking-where." Miles feigns gagging.

This conversation could continue for months if I don't stop it. I slash a hand in the air.

"I want to increase our whiskey producing facilities."

Jaxon slams his notebook shut and stands. "I'll get on it."

"Hold on," Rhett grumbles. "What are the costs involved?"

I grin. "There are costs but they'll be recovered in no time since I just closed a deal with the largest restaurant chain in the US to exclusively carry our whiskey."

"Whoo hoo!" Miles jumps to his feet. "Awesome news!"

"I bet Paisley will be impressed," Zane says.

"She might even forget about how you're a wimp who wears three-piece suits to a meeting on the island," Kai adds.

I frown. Paisley also made a comment about my suit. She's not impressed with anything to do with me. Not my clothes. Not my money.

To her, I'm the boy from high school she hates.

The question is – why does she hate me? What did I ever do to her?

We were friends once.

Chapter 5

"I should have veto power." ~ Paisley

PAISLEY

Maya peeks into my lab. "Are you ready? If we don't leave now, we'll be late."

I check the time. "We won't be late. It's a three-minute walk and the meeting isn't scheduled to begin for another fifteen minutes."

Chloe moves Maya to the side. "I want front row seats."

Of course, she does. If Chloe isn't the center of attention, she wants the chance to become the center of attention.

"I don't understand why I have to attend the meeting."

"This is ridiculous," Sophia mutters. "I'm not standing in the hallway." She barges past Maya and Chloe. "You are attending this meeting."

"But—"

"But nothing. All of us are going."

"I'm with you, Paisley," Nova mutters. "I don't understand why we have to attend this meeting."

Chloe gasps. "It's a meeting to decide how to proceed with the sexiest man of the island competition. Of course, we *have* to be there."

"Aren't you married to the sexiest man on the island?" I ask. She smiles. "I am."

"Nuh-uh. I'm going to marry the sexiest man on the island," Sophia protests.

They begin to bicker and I return my attention to my work. Maya sidles up to me. "Nice distraction but you aren't getting out of this."

"Fine." I stand and herd everyone out of my lab.

"I tried to stop them," Blossom hollers as we pass her desk.

"If the principal in high school couldn't stop us, you don't stand a chance," Chloe declares as she flounces past my assistant.

When we arrive at city hall, the meeting room is already crowded. Chloe scowls. "I want to sit in the front row."

And I want to hide in the back but it appears neither one of us is getting what they want today.

Sophia grins. "Oh look. Parker's here. Let's join her."

"I need the restroom." I pivot on my heel to escape but Maya and Nova each grab an arm and drag me forward.

"What are you doing? You don't want me to have an accident, do you?"

Nova giggles. "You have the biggest bladder of all of us."

"Do you remember the time we did the stake out outside of Hudson's house and she didn't pee once all night?" Maya asks.

"Probably because I wasn't doing shots of moonshine with you."

Nova's nose wrinkles. "Oh yeah. I forgot."

Maya giggles. "I didn't forget the way you tried to tackle the cheerleader when she left Hudson's place."

Nova sniffs and lifts her nose in the air. "Yeah, well, I'm engaged to Hudson now and we have a baby so little Miss Cheerleader can go for a short hike off a cliff."

They maneuver me until I'm sitting in between the two of them in the second row behind Chloe and Sophia. Why am I not surprised Chloe and Sophia managed to finagle front row seats?

"Is this seat occupied?"

I drop my chin to my chest at the male spoken question. Seriously? What is *he* doing here?

"Nope." Nova smiles at Eli. "Please, join us."

"Thanks. How have you been?"

Why didn't I bring earplugs? I have a supply of them at the lab. If I could plug my ears, I wouldn't have to listen to Eli speak. His gravelly voice causes tingles to erupt in places tingles have no business erupting when it comes to Eli, aka Enemy Number One.

"I'm good. And I've heard you're doing extremely well."

He chuckles. Ugh. How can a chuckle from a jerk sound this good? It's unfair. And plain wrong.

I eye the exit. Maya clamps a hand down on my thigh and leans close to whisper, "You're not going anywhere."

I narrow my eyes at her. "I can make all of your romance books disappear."

She giggles. "No worries. I have an e-reader now, too. Caleb bought me one as a surprise gift. He claims there's no more room for books in the house. He's silly. There's always room for more books."

Maya is obsessed with romance novels. If she's not working or hanging out with us, she has her nose buried in a book. Or, at least, she used to. Now she spends her free time with her fiancé. I'm happy for her. I am. Caleb fought his demons for her. And she's happy. She deserves it.

But I am not happy with how she's teamed up with the rest of our friends to tease me about Eli. I thought she'd ignore their attempts to matchmake me. I thought wrong.

Chloe glances behind her. "Oh, hey, Eli. I didn't expect you to be here."

He raises an eyebrow. "You didn't contact my assistant and ensure this meeting was on my agenda?"

I should have known. My friends and their matchmaking. They need to stop interfering in my business. If they knew what Eli had done, they'd... Hold on. They don't know. Maybe I should tell them. I scowl. Tell my friends about the biggest humiliation of my life? Nah. I'll pass.

Chloe bats her eyelashes at Eli. "Who? Me?"

He chuckles. "My mistake. It must have been another Chloe Summers."

She waves her left hand at him. "It's Chloe Fellows now."

"Congratulations. I heard you got married. I can't believe a man on Smuggler's Hideaway managed to tame the wild child."

"Lucas isn't a native smuggler."

"I call this meeting to order," the mayor, Lana, hollers from where she stands in front of the room. "There's one item on today's agenda – the sexiest man of the island competition."

Several people in the back catcall. The competition is a favorite among natives and visitors alike. Probably because it's required to kiss a man before you can cast your vote for him. Which is also why we're here today. The kissing requirement is under fire. As it should be.

"I'm afraid I've brought you here today under false pretenses."

At the mayor's announcement, the chatter in the room increases until it's nearly a roar.

"False pretenses?" Chloe rubs her hands together. "This is going to be fun."

Sophia bumps her shoulder. "Don't get too excited."

"Too late."

"Settle down!" Lana yells and quiet descends in the room.

"What's going on?" Chloe shouts. "What are these false pretenses?"

"My email said we need to discuss the kissing rule. And we need to. But there's a more pressing problem. Funds."

"Funds! What funds?" someone shouts from the back.

"Exactly. There aren't any funds for the end of the summer dance when we announce the sexiest man of the island."

Eli stands. "I'll pay."

"Typical billionaire," I mutter under my breath. "Always showing off their wealth."

He glances at me. Maybe I didn't mutter as quietly as I thought.

"I meant the distillery will sponsor the dance provided our beverages are exclusive."

I jump to my feet. "What about *Five Fathoms Brewing?* You can't have a party on Smuggler's Hideaway without our beer."

"You can co-sponsor."

"How would—

Maya tugs on my arm. "No, we can't. We can't afford it. The expansion into *Gourmet Corner* grocery stores throughout the US will use up all of our contingency funds."

Eli smirks. "*Buccaneer's Whiskey* will sponsor the entire event. No problem."

I glare at him. He had to add the 'no problem'? Supreme Jackass.

"Must be nice to be a billionaire and use your private funds for your little pet project."

"Pet project? Are you referring to my distillery as a pet project?"

"I didn't stutter, did I?"

"Considering *Five Fathoms* can't afford to sponsor maybe the brewery is the pet project."

I snort. "Pet project is an activity you engage in during your free time." I tap my chin. "For example, a distillery you only work at when you're not involved with your real job."

His nostrils flare. "The distillery is my real job."

"Dang it. I should have brought popcorn. This is the best entertainment," Chloe mutters.

"Here." Sophia hands her a bag of peanuts.

I grit my teeth at their act. "Can you two please behave?"

"Why?" Chloe asks as she chews her nuts. "This is fun."

I push my glasses up my nose as I contemplate how much trouble I would be in if I smacked her. Probably a lot. After all, she is married to a police officer.

"Why don't we put it to a vote?" the mayor asks.

"Put it to a vote?" I frown. "You'll actually allow an event to occur on Smuggler's Hideaway that isn't inclusive?"

Eli chuckles. "Your definition of inclusive is wrong."

Nova giggles. "Oh no, he didn't."

I cross my arms over my chest and meet his gaze. "Inclusive is defined as including all the items normally expected. Considering *Five Fathoms* beers are served at every bar and restaurant on Smuggler's Hideaway *and* the beers have been available at every festival on the island since our establishment, I do believe excluding *Five Fathoms* is not being inclusive."

"Here! Here!" Chloe lifts her hands in the air and peanuts rain down on her.

"I'm merely trying to help the island," Eli claims.

I raise an eyebrow. "Help the island or help your distillery?"

"I'm sorry, Paisley," Lana says before Eli can respond. "But without sponsorship of some sort, there aren't enough funds to proceed with the end of summer party. Considering the party brings in a ton of tourists, I don't want to cancel it."

"I don't understand why there aren't enough funds. Smuggler's Hideaway hosts numerous festivals. Where did the proceeds from these events go?"

Lana frowns. "To road construction after this past winter's unexpected snowstorm."

Dang it. I forgot about the snowstorm. I usually don't forget anything. But my brain goes on the fritz whenever I'm around Eli.

"I understand," I mutter and sit down.

Lana claps. "Excellent. The party will be sponsored by *Buccaneer's Distillery* and Paisley will join the party committee to help."

Wait. What?

I spring to my feet. "I didn't agree to join the committee."

Lana smirks. "You got volunteered."

"Fine," I grumble since it's impossible to fight Lana once her mind's made up. The mayor is a force to be reckoned with. Just ask her three ex-husbands.

"It's good you know when you're defeated," Eli says.

Asshole. He couldn't quietly accept his win and let it be? He has to remind everyone I'm the loser? Did I say asshole? I meant Grade A Asshole.

"I am never defeated. This is merely a setback."

He chuckles. "Whatever you need to tell yourself to sleep at night."

Sleep? I won't be sleeping at all until I devise the perfect plan to prank Eli. I could ask Chloe for help. She's a master pranker. But I want to do this one all on my own.

Eli will feel my wrath.

Chapter 6

"I'm not jealous of my brother. I have indigestion is all." ~ Eli

ELI

I glance up when Zane strolls into my office. "Pack it up. It's time to party."

I frown at him. "It's four o'clock."

"Exactly. We're late."

"Late? I don't have anything on my agenda." I reach for my phone but he snatches it away.

"Nope. No checking your phone. In fact," he stuffs my phone in his back pocket, "let's go without phones for an hour."

I glare at him. "I need my phone."

He rolls his eyes. "You don't *need* your phone. What you *need* is a drink."

I sigh. I'll never admit it to my brother, but he's not actually wrong. I could use a drink. It's been a long week between fighting with my brothers about how to expand the distillery and arguing with Paisley at the meeting.

I can never say the right thing to her. Whatever I say she interprets as me shoving my wealth in her face. And then I open my mouth and snark at her. I can't seem to help myself. She brings out the worst in me.

"You're softening. Come on. Let's go." Zane dances to the hallway.

I switch off my computer and follow him. Rhett is already waiting there. The way he's gazing at Dakota with longing in his eyes has my hackles rising. Those two are oil and water. Those two getting together will cause fireworks the distillery might not survive. I make a mental note to speak to Jennifer from *Apparoo* about writing up an anti-fraternization policy.

Jaxon rushes toward us. "Sorry, I'm late."

Late? My brow furrows. "Why does everyone but me know what's going on?"

Kai waves from the doorway. "Because you're never here."

Those words aren't meant to hurt but they sting, nonetheless. I've missed way too much of their lives. Between college and growing *Apparoo* into the multi-national business it is, I've spent way too little time with my brothers over the past decade. But I'm here now. And I plan to stay.

"You're never on time but suddenly we're having drinks and you are?"

Kai shrugs. "I have my priorities straight."

I approach Dakota. "If anyone calls—"

She shoos me away. "I'll deal with it. Get out of here and have a good time."

I want to invite her with us – she's an integral part of our team – but I don't dare. Alcohol and Dakota and Rhett is a combination I'm not ready for.

Zane urges me toward the exit. "Let's go. Let's go."

I scan the group. "Where's Miles?"

"He's meeting us at the *Rumrunner*."

"The *Rumrunner*?" The *Rumrunner* is in downtown Smuggler's Rest. I need to avoid the town and a certain inhabitant.

"Can't we go have a drink at the bar at the *Hideaway Haven Resort* instead?"

Kai shakes his head. "No way. The drinks there are overpriced."

"And it's boring," Zane adds.

My pulse quickens. It's Friday afternoon and my brothers are insisting we go drinking. This will not end well. At least the police cells on Smuggler's Hideaway have windows and proper beds. Ask me how I know.

"Boring's good."

Rhett nods in agreement. "Boring is safe."

Jaxon removes his glasses to pinch his nose. "I can't spend another night in jail. I have too much work to do."

Zane scowls at him. "It was one night years ago."

Kai bumps Jaxon's shoulder. "You're a workaholic. You need to have fun. Have a few drinks. Maybe get laid."

Jaxon rears back. "I don't… I mean… I could… But…"

Zane throws an arm over his shoulders. "Kai was joking."

Kai glances at me and mouths *No, I wasn't.*

I blow out a breath. Great. I'm going to spend the entire night trying to save Jaxon from his brothers.

"Welcome to the trenches," Rhett mutters.

We turn into the alley where the bar is a few minutes later. *Rumrunner* is a speakeasy and is supposed to be difficult to find. In reality, their social media channels blare their location to one and all. However, visitors do need to solve a riddle to get the password to enter.

Kai skips to the door and knocks. A small window opens and he waves. "It's us."

The door opens and the doorman ushers us inside.

"Hey, Trent," I greet.

"Good," he grunts. "You're here. Maybe you can keep your brothers in line."

Rhett snorts. "Impossible."

"Oh no." Jaxon groans.

Crap. Have my brothers already caused chaos? "What?"

He gestures to the banner hanging above the bar. *Find the Secrets of the Island Scavenger Hunt.*

"What are the chances I can gather the family together and escape?" I ask Rhett.

He indicates Miles who's sitting in a booth and waving a piece of paper at us. "None."

"I entered us as the Whiskey Raiders," Miles says when we join him.

I hold my hand out to Zane. "I need my phone back."

"You can't run away. We already paid our entry fee."

I wiggle my hand. "Someone needs to be able to transfer the money when it's time to bail you out of jail."

"Fair point." He slaps the phone in my hand.

Damn. I would have felt better if he denied needing bail money.

"It's better to let them loose for a while. We'll rein them in before chaos descends," Rhett says.

"Really? Before chaos descends?"

He shrugs. "I do my best."

"We are going to win this!" A woman in the booth behind me declares and my muscles seize.

Shit. I know her voice. I glance behind me to check. Yep, it's Chloe. And her entourage. My gaze catches Paisley's and she snarls at me. I whirl around away from her and return my attention to my brothers. All of whom are smirking.

"Do you want to switch sides with me?" Miles asks. "You can't gaze longingly at her all night long from your side."

I flip him off and he dissolves into laughter. Asshole.

"What are the prizes anyway?" Sophia asks behind me. I strain to listen to their conversation.

"A gift basket with goodies from *Buccaneer's Whiskey*. The basket includes bottles of whiskey, moonshine, and gin as well as a flask and mugs," Chloe says.

"*Buccaneer's Whiskey.* The owner of the distillery just loves to flaunt his wealth in everyone's face, doesn't he?" Paisley says.

Kai jumps to his feet and points to me. "The owner of the distillery is right here if you want to lodge a complaint in person."

Is it wrong to punch my brother? Mom would totally understand. I know she's wanted to punch Kai more than once. No one wants to wake up to a snake in your bed. Even if it is a rubber snake.

"All of us are shareholders in the business," I grit out.

Kai rolls his eyes. "I'm not stupid. I can do math."

"When I tutor him," Jaxon mutters, and Kai slaps his shoulder.

"While all of us have shares," Kai continues, "you're the majority shareholder."

"If I'm the majority shareholder, why didn't I know the distillery is sponsoring this scavenger hunt?"

"You're sponsoring this?" Paisley asks. She doesn't wait for a response. "I should have known. Any excuse to show off how wealthy you are to everyone else." She rolls her eyes. "We get it. You're a billionaire. Big deal."

Zane barks out a laugh. "I love you, Paisley."

I know he's joking but my body must not since my stomach dips as jealousy fills me and my fists clench with the desire to punch him.

While I'm wrestling with my control, a woman sashays to the booth. She bites her bottom lip and flutters her eyelashes at me. My body has no response. "Did I hear correctly? You're the owner of the distillery?"

"I'm out," Paisley says before shoving her friends out of the booth so she can stand. "CEO of Annoying," she mutters as she stomps past me.

My eyes are glued to her ass as she moves. What a glorious ass it is. I'd love to watch it bounce up and down as I sink into her. But Paisley has made herself perfectly clear. She hates my guts. I need to forget about her and move on.

The bartender sets a beer down in front of me.

"Hey, Harper," I greet. "How have you been?"

"I was much better before you lot showed up," she mutters before walking off.

I lift my beer to have a drink but the glass dissolves in my hand, and I end up with beer all over my pants.

"You're welcome," Paisley shouts from across the room.

Zane whistles. "Note to self. Never piss off Paisley."

I narrow my eyes on him. He needs to stop talking about her. He smirks as he holds up his hands.

"She's all yours, bro. I don't poach."

I scowl. Paisley isn't mine. As evidenced by my soaking wet pants.

Chapter 7

"If I close my eyes, I can pretend things could be worse." ~
Paisley

PAISLEY

I fist my hands on my hips as I scan the building.

"What do you think?" Maya asks. "Is it enough?"

I hope it is. It would break my heart to lose the brewery due to a hurricane. "We've done the most we can do. We've installed storm shutters, sealed the doors, and reinforced the roof."

Maya motions to where Nova, Sophia, and Chloe are working. "And they've trimmed all the trees and shrubs, cleared the gutters and drains, and anchored any loose items."

"We've done everything we can."

This isn't the first time we've prepped for a hurricane but it's the first time since the *Five Fathoms* brewery was built.

Maya squeezes my bicep. "If all else fails, we have hurricane insurance. Some very expensive insurance."

I force a smile. I know she's trying to reassure me but it's not working. I've been following the storm's path. We need a miracle for the hurricane to miss Smuggler's Hideaway.

Nova trudges over to us with Sophia and Chloe following her. "If we're done here, I should get going. Hudson needs all the help he can get with the resort."

My stomach dips. Here I'm worried about our brewery while Nova has much more to worry about. *Hideaway Haven Resort* and her home are right on the beach. Even if the hurricane manages to miss us, flooding near the beach is a given.

"Go." I urge her. "We've done as much as we can here."

She gives each of us hugs before hurrying off. "Be safe!" she shouts as she jumps into her car and speeds away.

"I'm off as well," Sophia says. "Flynn has been blowing up my phone. He wants me home safe."

She blows us kisses before leaving.

"Do you want to come home with me?" Maya asks.

My brow wrinkles. "Why?"

"Um." She bites her lip.

"Because you'll be alone," Chloe answers. She threads her arm through mine. "I'll be alone as well. Lucas is on duty until the storm passes. You're welcome to come home with me."

"You won't be alone. Your daughter will be with you."

"Natalia's fun. We have a bunch of games all ready for when the electricity goes out."

I unwind her arm from mine. "I'll be fine. This storm is an excuse to catch up on my reading."

Maya's eyes light up. "What are you reading? Anything super hot?"

Chloe laughs. "She's not reading one of your romance novels. She's probably reading some boring non-fiction book about the history of brewing."

Ha. Jokes on her. I've already read every book on the history of brewing I could find.

"I'm actually reading a biography." But I'm not telling them it's the biography of Jeremy Holland, the man who established *Apparoo* together with Eli.

"If you're sure?" Chloe asks.

"I'll be fine. I'm used to being alone."

Maya frowns at my reference to my family. She knows how it feels to be estranged from your family. But unlike her, I don't yearn for their love. I gave up on them long ago. Although, she doesn't yearn for her parents' love anymore since she now has Caleb.

A man strolls out of the brewery. Speaking of Caleb. He ensures the door is sealed up tight before making his way to us.

"I elevated as many appliances as I could and I tested the generator."

"Thank you for your help but shouldn't you be at the resort helping Hudson?"

Once Caleb was discharged from the Army, Hudson hired him as the chief of security at the resort.

"Nope. Hudson has it covered." He throws an arm around Maya's shoulders to bring her near. "Besides, there was no way I was being separated from Maya now."

Maya rolls her eyes. "Someone's a bit overprotective."

Caleb kisses her hair. "I finally have you. I'm not letting anything happen to you."

Maya melts into him. I feel a stab of jealousy. I want what they have. A man who supports me. A man who understands me.

"Welp! I'm off to kiss my sexy cop husband goodbye before going home to calm my daughter who has been yelling at her dad all day about how they should have moved somewhere without hurricanes."

Chloe waves before jumping on her bike and pedaling away.

"I'm off as well. There's nothing more to be done here," I say.

Maya and Caleb fall into step with me. "You sure you're okay by yourself?"

"I'm fine. Be safe," I say before turning in the opposite direction of them.

♥♥♥

Two days later

My heart is in my throat as I walk toward the brewery. Hurricane Isaac has come and gone. And he wreaked havoc in his wake.

There's no cell phone reception, and the electricity is out. I have no idea what to expect. Did *Five Fathoms Brewing* survive?

I glance around the street as I walk. Most of the houses appear okay. There are some trees down and debris litters the road but otherwise, there's no extensive damage.

But I know hurricane damage can vary widely – even on a small island. It's entirely possible this part of the island was unaffected but other areas experienced more extensive damage.

As I walk, I pick up debris and tree branches and place them on the side of the road. As much as a hurry I'm in to check on the brewery, I can't ignore the debris.

I reach the main street and scan the area. The sight fills my heart with hope. There's hardly any damage here at all. A few broken windows and some trash sprinkled on the street but nothing major.

My pace increases as I make my way to the brewery. If the businesses on the main drag are fine, maybe the brewery is, too.

"Wait for me!" Maya shouts.

I glance over my shoulder. She's running toward me.

"I really need to do more cardio," she says before bending over and gasping for breath.

"No Caleb?"

"He's on his way to the resort. Although he did make me promise to be safe."

I motion toward the street the brewery is on. "Shall we?"

We start walking but are stopped when another voice shouts for us to, "Hold up!"

This time it's Chloe running toward us with her daughter, Natalia.

"Shouldn't you be at home where your daughter is safe?" I ask when she reaches us.

"Lucas said the damage is minimal."

The spark of hope in my belly grows. "Let's hope he's right."

We continue to the brewery. When we arrive, Sophia is waiting with Nova next to her car.

"Hudson let you leave the resort?" I ask Nova.

"The resort is mostly fine. There's some flooding and damage to the landscaping but no structural damage."

"Great news! Let's hope *Five Fathoms* is as lucky," I say.

"The restaurant appears fine," Chloe says as we walk across the parking lot.

The bar and restaurant with the offices above are in a restored barn near the street. The brewery is across the parking lot in a separate building.

"You check out the restaurant. I need to check the brewery."

Chloe ignores me and follows me with the rest of our friends past the restaurant. As soon as the brewery comes into view, I gasp.

"NO!" I scream and run toward the structure.

"Shit! Shit! Shit!" Chloe chants as she chases me.

Sophia shackles my wrist to stop me from entering the brewery. "No. Wait until Flynn is here. He can ensure the building is structurally sound before you go inside."

"Structurally sound? The roof is missing!"

"All the more reason for you to stay here and wait," she says.

"I'll be careful," I claim as I remove an electric screwdriver from my backpack.

No one else tries to stop me as I remove the screws from the plywood protecting the door. Once all of the screws are out, they help me carry the plywood away.

I reach for the door and Maya squeezes my hand. "Whatever happens, it'll be okay."

She waits for my nod before releasing me. I enter the brewery and my jaw falls open. It's much worse than I expected. It's obviously been raining inside for two days.

Sophia plants herself in front of me. "I'm sorry. But I can't allow you to go any further. I don't want you to be electrocuted."

"The power's been off for nearly two days."

"I don't care."

I growl at her. "I care. This is my life. This is my passion. My dream. And it's been destroyed."

She places a hand on my shoulder. "It's my dream, too, Paisley."

"It's all of our dreams," Chloe adds.

"This is why we have insurance. We'll rebuild," Maya says.

"And how much time will elapse before the insurance money is deposited into our bank account? We may need years to rebuild. It's fine for all of you. You have partners you can rely on. I don't have anyone."

"Bullshit," Chloe mutters.

"What did you say?"

"I said bullshit. You're not alone. You have us."

I motion to the destroyed brewery. "I meant for income."

I didn't but income is as good an excuse as any.

Chloe's eyes flash. She knows I'm lying but to my surprise, she doesn't call me on it. "The bar and restaurant don't appear damaged. Yes, the beer sales are our major source of income but the bar and restaurant income will help us to get by until we can rebuild the brewery."

"But we don't have any *Five Fathoms* beer to sell at the bar and restaurant."

Maya clears her throat. "We just sent a big shipment to the resort. If Hudson agrees, we can recall the shipment."

"Hudson will agree. He'll do whatever I want." Nova winks.

"And I'll make sure Flynn puts us at the top of the list for construction work. All his projects are officially on hold until the brewery is rebuilt," Sophia says.

"We need the insurance money first."

She waves away my concern. "I have the money I was saving for my wedding."

I frown. "I can't allow you to use the money for your wedding."

"You," she stabs my chest, "aren't allowing me to do anything. I'm doing it. End of discussion."

I open my mouth to argue further but she herds me outside of the building with help from the rest of my friends.

"There." Nova says. "We have a plan."

"And everyone knows how much you love a plan," Maya adds.

I glance up at the missing roof of the brewery. I might love a plan but I love this brewery more. I finally found the one thing I'm passionate about and it was stolen from me.

My stomach falls as tears well in my eyes. It could've been worse. At least the restaurant is standing. The despair I'm feeling doesn't wane. Why couldn't the restaurant have been destroyed? And the brewery spared?

Chapter 8

ELI

"Wow." I study the distillery. If I hadn't personally experienced the hurricane, I wouldn't believe one happened based on what I'm seeing. "I can't believe it."

"There's been minimal damage," Rhett says.

"The effects of the hurricane shouldn't influence our production too much," Jaxon adds. "The expansion can continue as planned as well."

I run a hand down my face. "I can't believe how lucky we've been."

"Smuggler's Hideaway as a whole was lucky," Kai says.

"Not everyone," Miles mutters.

I slap his back. "I'm sorry about your surfboard business. I'll put in some calls today and get moving on the rebuild."

I'm not surprised the shack where he stores his surfboards and other equipment he uses to provide surfing lessons didn't survive the storm. I've been pushing him for years to build a more secure structure. But he wanted to do this business on his own with none of my money. I respected his motives and let him be.

"Other businesses were affected as well," Zane says.

"I'm certain they were. We'll help where we can."

Rhett and Jaxon nod in agreement while Zane's eyes sparkle.

"I bet there's a certain brewery you want to help first."

My muscles seize up at Zane's insinuation. "What brewery?"

It's a stupid question. There's only one brewery on the island.

"According to the smuggler's grapevine, the roof blew off the brewery."

Shit. A missing roof can cause a lot of damage. I whip out my phone to contact Paisley.

"Cell towers are still down," Rhett says. "They should be up and running within a day."

I shove my phone back in my pocket. I can't believe I forgot there was no service.

"I need to…" I wave toward the exit.

"Go on," Rhett says. "I've got things handled here."

"Say hi to Paisley for us," Kai hollers as I hurry out of the distillery. He chuckles but I ignore him in my haste to get to Paisley.

Is she okay? According to the smuggler's grapevine, no one was seriously injured during the storm. But some injuries aren't visible. If her brewery is destroyed, she's going to be wrecked.

I jump in my SUV and drive as fast as I can to *Five Fathoms Brewing*. Unlike the distillery, the brewery is located near the town of Smuggler's Rest.

The parking lot is crowded when I arrive. I scan the area for Paisley but I don't spot her amongst the crowd. There's a container for debris set up near the brewery and a steady file of people dropping debris into it. Damn. Those are the remnants of the roof.

I notice Nova standing near the container holding a baby in her arms.

She smiles as I near. "Hey, you. Everything okay at the distillery?"

"Yes. We got lucky."

Her smile dims. "We didn't."

"I'm sorry."

The baby in her arms cries and she jostles her. "Can you hold her for a moment?"

She doesn't give me a chance to respond before shoving the baby into my arms. "This is Iliana."

I glance down at the little girl. I haven't held a baby in my arms since Kai.

"You're good with her."

"You sound surprised."

"You're wearing a three-piece suit and shoes that probably cost more than my entire shoe collection and I'm married to a millionaire who enjoys treating me to new shoes."

I frown. "They're only clothes."

Her nose wrinkles. "They don't exactly scream smuggler, though, do they?"

"I guess not."

I thought Paisley was being bratty when she pointed out my clothes. But maybe she's right. Maybe my clothes make me appear to be an outsider on the island I grew up on. The island I consider home. The island I have no plans to ever leave ever again.

"Paisley's around back."

I don't bother lying and saying I'm not here for Paisley. What's the point?

I hand her Iliana. "She's a beautiful girl. Congratulations."

"Thank you," she murmurs but her attention is all on her baby girl. I don't blame her. She's precious. If I had a baby, I'd give her all of my attention, too.

I force those thoughts away and make my way around the building. I nearly gasp when I encounter the devastation back here. There are pieces of the roof everywhere.

I scan the area until I spot Paisley. My feet travel toward her before I realize I'm moving.

"Paisley," I call.

She stands up and spins toward me. Strands of her hair have escaped her ponytail and are matted to her face. She runs the back of her hand over her forehead to wipe away the sweat leaving a streak of dirt behind. Despite it all, she's never looked more beautiful.

"What do you want? Did you come to gloat?"

"Gloat?"

She plants her hands on her hips. "Your distillery didn't suffer any damage but the brewery is practically destroyed."

I frown. "And you think I would gloat about it."

She motions to my clothes. "You certainly didn't come to help in the outfit you're wearing."

"What do you need help with?"

She waves to the debris scattered on the ground. "What do you think?"

I remove my jacket and hang it on the lowest branch of the one tree left standing before rolling up my sleeves.

"I came to offer you a different kind of help, but I can do this, too."

She raises her eyebrows. The skepticism is plain to read on her face.

I grab a piece of wood from the ground. "Are you sorting materials? Or does everything go in the container together?"

She points to a pile of wood. "Wood goes there. Building materials go in the container."

I gather a few pieces of wood before carrying them to the pile. Paisley follows me the entire way.

"What did you mean about coming to offer a different kind of help?" she asks once I've dropped my load.

I go back to gathering wood while I contemplate how to answer.

"Well," she pushes when I don't speak.

I stand to face her. "The distillery wasn't damaged during the storm."

She scowls. "Thanks for the reminder."

"We have a lot of extra space as we're planning to expand production."

"Rub it in, why don't you?"

"I came to offer you the space for you to brew and produce *Five Fathoms* beer."

Her eyes widen and her jaw drops open. "I wish I could say I'm imagining things but I'm not prone to flights of fancy. And I know I'm not dreaming as my vision is always impaired while I dream. Perhaps my ears are due for a thorough cleaning."

"You don't need to have your ears cleaned."

"But why would you offer us space in your distillery? What do you get out of it?"

First of all, the offer was made to her. Without Paisley, the brewery wouldn't be on my radar. And, secondly, why does she assume I'm getting any benefit out of my offer?

"It's a friendly offer as a fellow smuggler."

"A fellow smuggler?" She waves toward my suit pants.

"Being well dressed doesn't mean I'm not a smuggler."

"When was the last time you've been to the beach?"

Ha. Joke's on her. "I was there this morning."

"You were?" She slides her glasses up her nose as she contemplates me. Understanding lights in her eyes and she snaps her fingers. "Of course. You were checking on Miles. How is his surfing shack?"

"Destroyed."

"How unfortunate. But it's not surprising. The structure was not hurricane proof."

"I agree but I'm not saying a word to him about it."

"Paisley!" a man shouts.

"Thanks for your help. Flynn needs me."

She walks off but I stop her with a question. "Aren't you going to consider my offer?"

"Why? So you can lord it over me about how you're a billionaire and your business is more successful than mine?" She shakes his head. "No thanks."

"I'm not lording my money over you."

"Okay," she says but she clearly doesn't believe me. "Thanks for your offer but I don't need a man to save me."

"I'm not trying to…" I trail off when she stalks away.

I growl. Stubborn woman. Why won't she accept my help? It could be months before the insurance company reviews their claim, let alone pays out.

She's letting her hatred of me cloud her vision. And why does she hate me anyway? We were friends once in high school. Is it pure jealousy?

I don't know but I'm making it my mission to find out.

Chapter 9

"I'm beginning to understand the appeal of stomping your foot in frustration." ~ Paisley

PAISLEY

I collapse in a booth next to Nova and her baby daughter, Iliana. Chloe sets a beer in front of me and I sip on it as I study the interior of the *Five Fathoms* restaurant.

"It looks good in here."

"We were lucky," Chloe says. "Besides some broken glass and general dirt and debris, there wasn't much damage."

While I've spent the day removing the remnants of the roof from the parking lot and surrounding area, Chloe and Maya have cleaned up the restaurant to get it ready to reopen as soon as possible. Which is a relief since we'll be relying on the revenue from the bar and restaurant for a while.

"I heard a rumor," Nova says as she bounces Iliana on her lap.

"I'm surprised Hudson allowed you to keep Iliana with you all day," I say since I'm afraid I know exactly what rumor she's referring to.

"Hudson does love his baby girl." Nova lifts Iliana in the air and kisses her cheeks with loud smacks.

"I want to know what this rumor is." Chloe's eyes sparkle with mischief.

Sophia juts her hand into the air. "Me too."

"Me three," Maya adds.

"Rumors can cause stress, anxiety, and physical and mental strain."

"She's cute. Isn't she cute?" Chloe bumps Sophia's shoulder who nods in agreement.

"I'm not being cute. I'm merely stating how rumors can have negative impacts."

Nova clears her throat. "Why don't we find out if this rumor is true?"

"Yeah." Sophia leans close.

Chloe bobs her head. "Good idea."

"What's the rumor?" Maya asks and I bite my lip before I scowl at her.

Maya has always been shy but since she's been living with Caleb, she's becoming bolder. I'm proud of her but is it too much to ask for her to crawl back in her shell until Eli leaves the island? And, yes, Eli will leave the island eventually. Smuggler's Hideaway can't hold the attention of a billionaire.

Nova clears her throat. "Eli offered Paisley space in his distillery to brew in until her brewery is up and running again."

Maya squeals while Sophia and Chloe give each other high fives.

"False," I say and everyone focuses their attention on me.

"But I heard—"

I narrow my eyes on Nova. "Were you eavesdropping on my conversation?"

She rolls her eyes. "Duh."

"You're not a very good eavesdropper."

She rears back with a gasp. "How dare you!"

"Eli didn't offer *me* space in his distillery for *my brewery*. He offered *Five Fathoms* space to brew *Five Fathoms* beer."

Nova rolls her eyes. "Oh, please. If you weren't around, Eli wouldn't have bothered rushing to the brewery like he was a pirate with a mermaid on his ass today."

"This is excellent." Sophia rubs her hands together. "When will you start?"

Chloe wiggles her eyebrows. "And by start, we mean when will you abandon your clothes and get busy in the sheets?"

Cold invades my body as sadness fills me. I would love to 'get busy in the sheets' with Eli as Chloe put it. But Eli wants nothing to do with me. He made himself perfectly clear in high school.

"I didn't accept his offer."

My statement is met with stunned silence. And gaping mouths.

I nearly smile. It's not easy to stun my friends. Not even when Sophia's mom caught me watching an orgy film were they this stunned.

"I'm…" Sophia trails off. I've never rendered her speechless before.

Chloe stares at me with wide eyes. "You said no?"

Maya's nose wrinkles. "I don't understand."

Nova chuckles. "I do."

I push my glasses up my nose as I confront her. "I highly doubt you understand."

"Oh, I understand." I open my mouth to explain but she wags her finger at me. "Don't you dare go sprouting some facts to supposedly back up your refusal."

I snap my mouth closed. I was planning to explain how having a brewery in a distillery facility wasn't as simple as it sounds.

"You're scared. Plain and simple. Scared."

I narrow my eyes on her. "What am I scared of?"

"Love," Maya says. "You're afraid of love."

I bristle. "I am not afraid of love. Why would I be afraid of love?"

"I know. I know." Chloe bounces in her seat. "Because every person who was supposed to love you, hurt you."

This is what I get for having close friends who know everything about me. They use the information against me at the most inconvenient of times.

"Evil stepsisters? Check!" Sophia makes a checkmark in the air. "Asshole ex-boyfriend? Check!"

Chloe elbows her. "You forgot wicked stepfather."

"Wicked stepfather? Check!"

"This has nothing to do with my family," I grumble.

"Oh." Sophia bats her eyelashes and feigns innocence. The woman hasn't been innocent since second grade when she punched a boy for pulling her hair. "Why did you refuse Eli's offer of help in our time of need?"

Our time of need? Damn. This isn't good.

"We haven't discussed payment. Maybe *Five Fathoms* can't afford his help," I claim.

Maya frowns. "Try again."

Dang it. As the financial manager, Maya knows we'd be able to get an emergency loan in this situation.

"Maybe he wants payment in kind anyway." Sophia wiggles her eyebrows.

Nova checks her watch. "Out with the real reason. I need to be home soon or Hudson will scour the island searching for me."

I contemplate another delaying tactic but it wouldn't be fair to make Hudson worry. Nova's fiancé is overprotective but he also has the right to be worried when Nova and his daughter are gone for this long after a hurricane devastated the island.

I sigh. "I don't need a man to save me."

In particular, I'll be damned if I let Eli save me. Mr. Billionaire with his three-piece suits can take a hike in the ocean. Those expensive leather loafers would be ruined in seconds.

Maya reaches across the table to squeeze my hand. "Don't let pride get in your way of accepting help."

I snatch my hand away. "It's not my pride. *Five Fathoms* is a woman owned business. I don't want a man to sweep in and save us."

Sophia blows out a breath. "Okay. We won't allow the patriarchy to save us."

Chloe drums her fingers on the table. "I guess I could let some of the staff go."

Maya nods. "After the brewery, personnel are our highest cost. Maybe I should take a pay cut as well."

"You're not taking a pay cut unless I take one, too," Nova says.

"But you have the baby. You need the cash."

Nova snorts. "I also have a husband who's a millionaire. I'll be fine."

"I'll be fine, too," Chloe adds. "Lucas has a job with benefits. He earns enough for the both of us."

"Same here," Sophia says. "Flynn's business is growing like gangbusters."

"And Caleb has a job at the resort now. I don't need as much income," Maya says.

I glare at my friends. "You're not funny."

"What do you mean?" Maya asks, the picture of innocence.

"No one's pay is being cut." I can't allow them to lower their salaries. Especially since I can't afford to lower mine. There's only one solution. "I'll accept Eli's help."

Cheers erupt but I growl to stop their celebration with a hand in the air. "But if I hear one word about matchmaking me with Eli, I will get my revenge."

Chloe pretends to zip her lips. "You won't hear one word."

"And you won't pull any pranks to force us to get together."

"Define prank," Sophia says.

"To play a practical joke or perform a mischievous act."

She frowns. "Your definition is really broad."

On purpose. Because I know my friends. They're trouble-makers to the bone.

"You asked for a definition. I gave you one."

"My bad. I should have known better than to ask."

The door bangs open and Hudson strolls inside. "Uh oh," Nova mutters. "My time is up."

I scooch over to allow her out of the booth. Before she has the chance to stand, Hudson is there taking the baby from her and helping her up with a hand on her elbow.

My chest tightens as a wave of envy hits me. I want what they have. A loving family. But it's not to be. And not because I'm afraid of love. I'm not afraid. But I have learned my lesson. Love is not for me.

"Let us know how your meeting with Eli goes," Nova says as she waves goodbye.

Eli. More proof love is not for me. Not after what he did. And how he acted afterwards. His nicknaming me *Paisley the Perpetual Know It All* made his position perfectly clear.

Chapter 10

"Did I say I want to own a business with my brothers? I was mistaken." ~ Eli

ELI

Dakota skips into my office with a huge smile on her face.

I groan. "What did you do now? Please tell me you didn't put salt in Rhett's coffee again. The last time he threw the coffee maker across the room. It took a week for the replacement coffee pot to arrive. I can't survive without coffee."

She clasps her chest. "Me? Put salt in Rhett's coffee? I wouldn't dare. He's my superior."

I snort. "Which is why you are demure around him and never give him shit."

She bats her eyelashes. "I would never give anyone shit."

I chuckle. "You are full of shit."

"I guess I won't tell you who's here to see you then." She makes as if to leave but I stop her.

"Dakota, who's here?"

"It's me." Paisley strolls into my office. "I'm sorry to disturb your fun."

Her eyes narrow on Dakota. Hold on. Is Paisley jealous of Dakota? Maybe Paisley does care. Maybe she doesn't hate me. Maybe the lady doth protest too much.

"Don't you worry. I have another Raider brother to bother." Dakota winks before shutting the door behind her.

Paisley stares after her. "Another brother to bother? Are you sharing her?"

She's adorable when she's confused. Her nose scrunches up and her pretty pink lips purse. I want to run my tongue along her lips until she opens on a sigh. I'd thrust my tongue into her mouth and taste her. I've spent years wondering how she tastes.

"Dakota's teasing," I explain.

Paisley studies me for a moment before shrugging as if it's all no bother to her one way or another. She can't fool me. But I let it go. For now.

I stand and round my desk. "Have a seat." I motion to a chair as I lean against my desk. "What brings you to *Buccaneer's Whiskey & Distillery*?"

She steps in front of the chair but she doesn't sit. Not my Paisley. She's too stubborn to allow herself to sit while I'm standing. Usually, stubborn people drive me crazy but not Paisley. She drives me crazy but in a way I could easily become addicted to.

She fiddles with the hem of her t-shirt but when she notices me watching, she stuffs her hands in her pockets. "I've come here to discuss the possibility of *Five Fathoms* brewing beer in your facility."

I can't stop the smile from spreading across my face. If Paisley is near, I can grind her down until she tells me why she hates me.

"Don't gloat."

I hold up my hands. "Not gloating. But I am relieved you're accepting my help."

"Relieved?"

"It would be a shame if the bars and restaurants of Smuggler's Hideaway were unable to carry *Five Fathoms* beer."

Her face is full of mistrust but I ignore it. She's being forced to accept help from her enemy. Her pride must be hurt. I understand how pride can get in the way of help.

My brother, Miles, is the perfect example. His stubbornness makes me want to shove one of his surfboards up his ass until he learns to listen.

She straightens her back. "We need to discuss payment."

"Payment?"

She waves her hand. "Payment for the use of your facilities. In addition to rent, there will be utilities and water and—

My growl cuts her off. "You are not paying."

She fists her hands on her hips. "I'm not accepting charity."

"What's wrong with accepting help when you need it?"

Her nostrils flare. Uh oh. I poked the beast. Considering how her cheeks flush and nose scrunches making her usually pretty face appear beyond gorgeous, I may poke the beast more often.

"You're not being charitable. You're rubbing my nose in your wealth."

I'm about sick and tired of her claiming I'm showing off my wealth.

"How?"

She slides her glasses up her nose. "How what?"

"How am I rubbing your nose in my wealth?"

She flings her arm wide to indicate the distillery. "You have this fancy schmancy distillery and our brewery is merely a microbrewery."

"Your microbrewery closed a deal to supply one of the largest grocery chains in the US."

She rears back. "How do you know?"

"It was all over the financial news."

She drops her chin to her chest. "Oh."

My fingers inch to pinch her chin and lift her face to force her to meet my gaze but I cross my arms before I can give in to the temptation.

"*Five Fathoms* isn't some unknown microbrewery. And I didn't offer you space in the distillery because I feel sorry for you. I offered you space because we have it and you're a smuggler. Smugglers help other smugglers out."

The stiffness leaks out of her shoulders. "It's easy to forget you're a smuggler."

I ignore her comment. She's not the only one who's mentioned how much I don't resemble a smuggler recently. I need to work on it. But it's a concern for later.

"Let me do this for you now. When your brewery is back up and running, we can discuss some kind of repayment."

"You're not doing this for me. You're doing it for the brewery."

I clear my throat. "Of course. I misspoke."

I didn't misspeak. I am doing this for her. But she doesn't need to know how much I long for her. Especially not considering how she hates my guts.

"Do you want a tour of the facilities?" I motion to the door.

Her eyes light up. I knew she'd want a tour. Paisley is as interested in the actual mechanics of the production as Jaxon is.

She clears her throat. "I believe a tour would be handy. I can plan out where to put equipment."

I duck my chin to hide my amusement at her attempt to tone down her excitement. She's cute when she's excited. I wish I could make her excited more often. And not merely intellectually excited.

I open the door and Kai practically falls into the room. I glare at him. "How old are you?"

"Uh oh. Eli is getting senile in his old age. Do you remember my name at least?"

I grit my teeth. "Don't make me smack you in front of company."

He waves to Paisley. "Hello, brewer girl."

I move to block his view of her but Paisley responds before I have the chance. "Brewer woman. A girl is a female child or adolescent."

He salutes her. "My apologies. Brewer woman, how are you?"

"I've been better."

He frowns. "I'm sorry about the brewery." He opens his arms. "Do you want a hug?"

I shove him and he falls to the floor while laughing.

"You shouldn't shove your brother."

I raise an eyebrow at Paisley. "And you never shoved your friends in high school?"

"Nova deserved it. Her eavesdropping on Hudson caused me to be late for my AP test in Chemistry."

"Yes. Let's pretend it only happened once." I chuckle. "You forget I was in your grade in high school. I was a witness to all of your shenanigans."

Kai sits up. "Shenanigans? Tell me more."

I ignore him and motion down the hallway. "The distillery is this way."

Rhett steps out of his office. "Did she agree?"

I snort. "Don't pretend you haven't been leaning against the wall with a glass to your ear for the past hour."

"Using a glass doesn't work," he claims.

"Actually," Paisley says. "A glass pressed against the wall focuses sound waves into a small area. If the shape of the glass is a curved cup-like surface, it can direct sound waves more effectively to your ear."

Rhett's mouth drops open. "Paisley is a female version of Jaxon."

I growl. "Do not make fun of Paisley."

"Why not? You used to make fun of her all the time in high school."

I was teasing her. Not making fun of her. There is a difference.

"Yeah. Well. We're not in high school anymore."

I place a hand on Paisley's lower back to guide her away from my idiot brothers and toward the distillery. She shivers and my blood heats.

How I'd love to move my hand from her lower back to her ass. Her ass is magnificent. My cock hardens and lengthens as ideas of what I could do to Paisley's ass flit through my mind.

"Ground Control to Major Eli," Jaxon says and I realize I'm standing in the entryway to the distillery staring into space.

I force my attention back to the present. "Jaxon, have you met Paisley? Jaxon is our master distiller. Paisley will be joining us as she's the master brewer for *Five Fathoms Brewing*."

"Nice to meet you," Jaxon says. "I'd love to pick your brain about hops sometime."

They shake hands and I have to stop myself from pulling her away from his touch. I need to get this obsession with Paisley under control.

She drops his hand and steps back from him. Or maybe not. Maybe I need to stop obsessing and make a move.

Chapter 11

"Rome can't be built in a day? Watch me." ~ Paisley

PAISLEY

Dakota meets me at the entrance to the distillery. She dangles a set of keys from her fingers. "These are yours."

"Thank you." I try to sound grateful but jealousy is clouding my vision and causing the words to get stuck in my throat. Eli obviously cares for Dakota in a way he will never care for me.

She tilts her head to study me. "You don't have to worry you know."

I don't have to worry? She's wrong. I've drafted a comprehensive list of things I need to worry about.

Will the mash and lauter tuns I ordered arrive today as agreed? Is the water filtration system at the distillery sufficient? Is there proper drainage, ventilation, and space for my equipment? Is there adequate electrical supply to power equipment? And what about—

"I mean about Eli."

I stop scrolling through my mental list and force my attention to Dakota. "Eli? What about Eli?"

"There's nothing happening between us."

I feel my cheeks heat but I pretend I'm not embarrassed. "I don't understand why you're telling me this."

"Eli and I banter but I have no interest in him. And he has no interest in me. I think I know why now."

My brow furrows. Is she inferring Eli is interested in me? The only interest Eli has in me is waving his success in my face. It's of no consequence. Eli is not on the list of topics I wish to discuss with a virtual stranger.

I need to extricate myself from this conversation but I don't know how. Usually, I'd walk away but she's standing in front of the door holding my set of keys.

"Thank you for being frank."

I hold out my hand and she drops the keys in them. "Have fun."

She strolls away toward the offices of the distillery. When she's out of sight, I turn to the door and unlock it. I step inside and switch on the light.

I gasp. The distillery facility is no longer one massive room. A wall now separates the facility into two distinct areas. I discussed the need to separate the brewing and distilling areas into two zones, but I didn't think Jaxon would have walls built.

How did he manage to have walls built in the week since I accepted Eli's offer to use his facilities? Sophia's fiancé, Flynn, is the main contractor on the island but he never mentioned anything to me.

"Does the setup meet your requirements?" Eli asks from behind me and I startle.

I wait until my heart calms down before facing him. "Yes. Thank you. Please thank Jaxon for me."

"Why would I thank Jaxon?"

I motion behind me. "Because he set this up for me."

"No, he didn't."

"But Jaxon is the master distiller in charge of the facility."

"He is but he's not the one who made sure your incredibly detailed list of requirements was met."

I'm confused. Is there a facility manager I don't know about? "He wasn't?"

"I handled everything personally."

I'm surprised. I assumed he didn't have time. I assumed he delegated most of his work. And...I need to stop assuming.

"Thank you. How did you get the walls built within a week?"

He smirks. "I know a contractor on the island."

I frown. "Flynn didn't tell me."

"I asked him not to."

"Why?"

"I wanted to surprise you."

"Mission accomplished. I'm surprised."

"Good. Now." He rubs his hands together. "How can I help?"

My brow furrows. "You're going to help me set up the equipment?"

He opens his arms wide. "I'm dressed to help."

For the first time, I notice what he's wearing. Worn jeans and a t-shirt with the logo of *Buccaneer's Whiskey* on it. Huh. He has jeans he's worn often enough for them to have faded?

He should wear these clothes more often. Don't get me wrong. Eli in a suit is a thing of beauty but in jeans? He looks good enough to eat. Which I won't be doing.

He checks his watch. "Shall I open up the garage doors? Your first delivery should arrive soon."

The rest of the day flies by as delivery after delivery arrives. I direct everyone where to place the mash and lauter tuns, the brew kettle, the fermenters, the beer tanks… The list goes on and on.

When we founded *Five Fathoms Brewing,* we didn't set up all the equipment in one day. It was a gradual growth as we went from brewing in my garage to opening the restaurant to building the brewery.

"I'm calling it a day," Eli says as he walks into the storeroom where I'm putting away the brewing ingredients.

"Thanks for your help," I say without bothering to look up from my work.

"No, Paisley. I'm calling it a day for everyone."

My hands freeze, and I glance over my shoulder at him. "Are you kicking me out?"

He runs a hand down his face. "No, I'm trying to make sure you don't fall over from exhaustion."

Fall over from exhaustion? What is he talking about?

"It's after nine. You've been here since seven."

I motion to the other areas of what is now our brewing facilities. "So has everyone else."

"Everyone else went home more than an hour ago."

My brow wrinkles. "They did?"

He chuckles. "Chloe came in here to say goodbye to you."

"I must have been distracted."

"Understandable. You're trying to build the brewing facilities in one day."

"I don't have much of a choice. Between the loss of production over the past two weeks and the cost of the new equipment – not to mention the cost to rebuild our old brewery – we need to begin production again as fast as possible. Oh, and I almost forgot whatever you charge us for rent."

I'm nearly hyperventilating when I finish. The pressure to begin brewing to ensure we are earning money again sits heavy on my shoulders.

"Hey." Eli steps close to grasp my hand. "Everything will work out."

I yank my hand from his. "Easy for you to say. You have money and a family to fall back on. I have me."

"I understand. I didn't always have money and my family."

"You might not have always been a billionaire, but you've always had your brothers."

"True. But I'm the oldest. When we were growing up, I was the one they relied on."

I knew Eli was the oldest but, "Why would they need to rely on you?"

He glances away. "My dad wasn't around."

Oh, right. His dad left when he was in high school. "What about your mom?"

"Mom worked two jobs to get food on the table."

"Your dad didn't pay child support?"

He snorts. "My dad disappeared."

I squeeze his hand but release it before I can enjoy the feel of his skin on mine. "I'm sorry."

"I wasn't trying to make this about me. I was merely trying to show you I understand how it feels to have the pressure on your shoulders."

I study him. I never thought of Eli as someone who felt pressure. Maybe I need to view him in a new light. Maybe I need to let go of what happened in high school.

I wasn't exactly the most mature individual in my teen years either. Case in point? I may have enjoyed it a bit too much when my stepsisters were forced to go to school with green teeth after I put food coloring in their toothpaste.

"Anyway." Eli dangles two beers in front of me. "I brought us supplies."

I swipe a beer from him. "This better be a *Five Fathoms* beer."

"I wouldn't dare offer any other beer."

"Come on." He ushers me out of the storage room to the office where we sit facing each other.

"I can't believe you gave me an office." And what an office it is. It's much nicer than the one I have... er... had at *Five Fathoms.*

"You need somewhere to work. You can't be on the floor all the time."

He sips from his beer and I watch as he swallows. The sight of his Adam's apple bobbing as he swallows has me thinking of other things he could taste and swallow.

I drink my beer before I say anything inappropriate such as ask him to remove his clothes. Bad idea.

"Are you happy with what you accomplished today?"

I blow out a breath. "I wanted to get more done."

He scowls. "You've literally worked your fingers to the bone."

I hold up my hand. "I still see skin and muscles over the bone."

He chuckles. "You know what I mean. There's only so much you can do in a day."

"I don't know. I prefer to think of myself as a superwoman who can do anything."

"Superwoman? Do you have a costume?"

I wave a hand over my jeans and t-shirt. "Do you not approve of my outfit?"

"There's nothing wrong with it but I wouldn't mind a chance to see you in a bustier with a little skirt."

I laugh but sober when I realize he isn't joking. Those striking blue eyes are full of heat as he stares at me.

No, no, no. I'm imagining things. Eli made himself perfectly clear in high school. He wants nothing to do with me.

"Bras are uncomfortable enough. A bustier would be torture."

His gaze drops to my breasts and I tighten my hold on my beer to stop myself from covering my chest with my hands.

Why, oh why, did I say anything about bras and bustiers?

"Plus, bare legs aren't safe in a production facility."

His gaze snaps back to my face and he smirks. "Wouldn't want anything bad to happen to those legs."

Those legs? I'm confused. Why is he being nice? Why is he joking with me? Why isn't he being an asshole?

Was I wrong about him? Is Eli not an asshole? Maybe I overreacted about what happened in high school? Maybe he doesn't want me the way I wanted him back then but does his past behavior make him an asshole in the present?

Rotten rum. I need to stop considering Eli Enemy Number One and open myself to the possibility I was wrong.

And if there's one thing I hate more than Eli Raider, it's being wrong.

Chapter 12

"I will not let a coffee machine defeat me." ~ Eli

ELI

I'm not surprised there's a light on in Paisley's office when I arrive at *Buccaneer's Whiskey.* No matter how early I arrived at work this past week, Paisley was already here. And she's here when I finish work, too.

Is she doing okay? She must be exhausted. I'll make her a coffee and bring it to her. It's as good an excuse as any to check on her.

Plan in place, I fold out of my SUV and head inside.

The offices of the distillery are dark when I enter. Not strange considering it's barely six a.m. My brothers and the rest of the staff usually don't arrive until around eight. Although Kai is always late, Zane comes and goes at will, and Miles often doesn't show up at all.

I can't complain. Zane is a master at marketing. And Miles did warn me he wouldn't be at the distillery often when we founded the company.

I dump my briefcase in my office before making my way to the break room. I prepare a cup of coffee for Paisley the way I know she drinks it. Strong with lots of sugar but no milk.

I hum as I traverse through the offices to the distillery. I pass Jaxon's office but he isn't in yet before reaching Paisley's.

"Good morning," I call as I enter.

Paisley jumps in her chair and clutches her chest. "You scared me."

I lift the coffee up in the air. "I bring you replenishments."

She reaches for the cup. "I could use a hit of caffeine."

I hand her the coffee making sure our fingers touch. A jolt of excitement rolls through me at the feel of her skin. The pads of her fingers are surprisingly soft considering how much she works with her hands.

I can't help but wonder how soft the rest of her skin is. It's a question I've spent quite a bit of time considering while laying in my bed with my cock in my hand. My cock twitches in reminder and I clear my throat before I end up getting hard.

Paisley sips on her coffee and moans. Damn. I want to hear her moan when she's sipping from my lips, not coffee. There is no chance of me not getting hard now.

"What are you working on?"

She rips her glasses off and flings them on the desk. "The scheduling. Coordinating the brewing, fermentation, packaging, and cleaning schedules shouldn't be this hard."

I chuckle. "Except you'd rather be playing around with new recipes or getting your hands dirty with the actual brewing."

She narrows her eyes on me. Without her glasses on, those hazel eyes of hers are even more gorgeous. "How do you know?"

"Because I know you, Lace."

She nabs her glasses and sets them back on her face. "Lace? You don't know me well if you can't remember my name."

The term of endearment slipped out. "I know you prefer to get your hands dirty rather than sit behind a computer all day."

She raises an eyebrow.

"I remember in biology class none of your friends would dissect the frog as assigned and you ended up dissecting five of them. One for you and one for each of your friends."

She narrows her eyes on me. "It wasn't cheating."

I raise my hands. "Of course not. Paisley Bardot would never cheat."

She sniffs and lifts her nose in the air. It's adorable. "Dang right, I wouldn't. I made my friends recite all the parts of a frog's anatomy before I agreed to help with their dissections."

"You and your friends always were troublemakers."

She scowls. "I'm not a troublemaker."

"And you didn't cover the social science teacher's desk with yellow sticky notes with drawings of a penis on them either?"

"He shouldn't have said sex education was a waste of time."

"The drawings were very accurate." We were fourteen at the time. How did she know the anatomy of a penis at such an early age? Especially when the teacher refused to teach us the sex education curriculum?

"I traced the drawings from an anatomy book I checked out in the library."

I grin. "I should have known. You practically lived in the library."

"It was the only place where I could get some peace from Chloe, Sophia, and Nova."

"I can't believe they've settled down."

She snorts. "Don't let them fool you. Being engaged – or married in Chloe's case – hasn't settled them down one bit."

I lift my coffee cup and realize it's empty. I stand. "You want another coffee?"

She pushes away from her desk. "I'll go with you."

"Why are you here this early?" she asks as we travel through the building.

"Working. The same as you," I say as I open the door to the break room and usher her inside. "Have a seat I'll make you a coffee."

She sits down. Her eyes widen as she studies the room.

"What is it?"

"This break room is over the top."

I scan the room. It's nothing special. Sure, the tables and chairs are luxurious but what's the sense in having a break room with uncomfortable chairs? You can't have a proper break if you're uncomfortable.

"I want everyone to be comfortable, so they can rest during their breaks."

She points to the shelf of glasses. "And they need baccarat crystal to rest?"

"Those were a gift. Since I wasn't planning on using them in my home, I brought them here."

"Already too much baccarat crystal at home?" she teases.

"Nah. I break shit too often. No fancy crystal for me."

"You break shit?"

"Correction. My brothers come over and decide to play hot potato with my stuff."

She giggles. "Now there's an explanation I believe."

"My brothers are shit stirrers."

"They're nearly as bad as my friends."

"Do not tell them that. They'll take it as a challenge."

"As would Chloe and Sophia."

"We should probably keep them apart."

She nods. "Good idea."

I return my attention to the coffee machine. I place Paisley's cup under the dispenser and hit the espresso button. But, instead of coffee filling her cup, water spurts out of the machine straight at me.

I slap my hands at the water in an attempt to stop the flow. But water continues to soak me until Paisley unplugs the machine.

"What did you do?" she asks.

I scowl at the machine. "Nothing. This machine hates me."

"An inanimate object hates you?"

"Yep." I nod. "It's possessed by the devil."

She giggles and I glare at her. She holds up her hands as she backs away. "Sorry. I'm just a little surprised by Eli Raider claiming a coffee machine is possessed by the devil."

I grab a towel and pat my suit jacket to dry it. "I'm going to have to dry clean this suit."

"If you wore jeans and a t-shirt, you wouldn't have to worry about the dry cleaner."

I frown. "Do you not approve of suits?" She complains about my clothes a lot.

"Suits are fine. But we live on an island. Even the mayor wears shorts and flip-flops."

"Because Lana is a nut."

"True but she's not wrong in her choice of attire for an island environment. The expected high temperature for today is eighty."

I toss the towel on the counter since drying myself is a waste of my time. I need to change my outfit. It's a good thing I keep a spare suit in my office. "The heat doesn't bother me much since I don't get outside often."

"I self identify as a workaholic and I get outside."

"When?" I push her. There's no way she has time to go outside.

"I go for a walk at lunch every day."

Now I understand why I can never find her when it's time to eat. I thought she was hiding from me.

"It lowers my blood pressure, gets the heart pumping, relieves stress, and helps to prevent weight gain amongst other benefits."

I rake my gaze over her body. "You don't have to worry about gaining weight."

"Everyone has to worry about gaining weight at a certain age."

I chuckle. "You're thirty. Not sixty."

She slides her glasses up her nose. "Nearly thirty-one."

I bark out a laugh. "I misspoke. You're obviously an old lady."

She nudges me to move. "Get out of the way. I need to fix this machine."

"I'll fix it."

She raises an eyebrow. "You're going to fix the machine you believe is possessed by the devil?"

"Better me than you to be cursed to spend an eternal life in hell with the Prince of Darkness."

"Lucky for me, I don't believe in the devil."

She winks and my heart flutters. She's laughing and joking with me. Maybe she doesn't hate me anymore. Maybe I should ask why she hated me before.

"I'm serious, Mr. Billionaire. Out of my way. I've got this."

And maybe I shouldn't push my luck. At least, not yet.

I'm slowly insinuating myself into Paisley's life. Day by day. Coffee by coffee. Joke by joke. She's getting used to me. It won't be long before she'll forget all about my money and her previous hatred of me.

And then I'll pounce.

Chapter 13

"Tease me all you want but cross the line to bullying and you'll regret it." ~ Paisley

PAISLEY

"I'm excited." Chloe skips toward the entrance to Mermaid Mini Golf. "I'm going to win. Again."

"Ha! No, you won't." Sophia chases after her.

Nova slings one arm over my shoulders and one arm over Maya's. "I'm just glad to get away from Mr. Overprotective for a few hours."

"You love Hudson and you know it," Maya says.

Nova grins. "I do. It's true. And you love Caleb."

"Never said I didn't."

I snort. "Except for the twelve years you were pen pals and claimed you were only friends."

"I was mistaken."

"Mistaken. Sure." I wink. I switch the subject before her face becomes red enough to light up the island. "I'm glad we managed to arrange an evening to play mini golf again."

We used to play once a month. And by play, I mean drink beer, do shots of whiskey, and generally forget about the actual miniature golf part of the evening. But since my friends have fallen in love, they don't have as much free time.

I expected this to happen. I dreaded the day in fact. Since I don't ever plan to fall in love – learned my lesson there – I knew I'd end up alone at some point. Especially since I don't have a family I care to spend time with.

My so-called family can fall off a cliff for all I care. Actually, I do care. In fact, I'll help push them.

Nova nods in agreement. "We need to make time for each other. Otherwise, the years will fly by and before we know it, Iliana will be graduating from high school."

"Where's your putter?" Chloe asks when we reach her.

I don't play golf but I am serious about winning miniature golf, which is why I have a putter. Or, rather, I used to.

"It was in my office."

Her face falls. "I'm sorry. I'm a cow for reminding you of the brewery."

"It's okay. I can hardly forget the brewery was destroyed by a hurricane when I had to relocate the entire brewing facility to another location."

"Another location?" Sophia snorts. "She's cute. She thinks if she doesn't mention Eli, we won't either."

It will be difficult to convince my friends – who for some reason think they're matchmakers – to not discuss Eli. But I have an excellent idea of a distraction. I lift the whiskey bottle I brought with me. "I purloined provisions."

Chloe's brow wrinkles. "Purloined?"

"It's a fancy way of saying steal," Maya says. "Heroes are always purloining things they shouldn't in historical romance."

"I'm surprised you still have time to read romance since you're now shacked up with Caleb," Nova says.

"It's impossible to have sex all the time." Maya's eyes widen when she realizes what she said. Her cheeks darken and she slaps a hand over her mouth.

Chloe barks out a laugh. "You've obviously tried."

I hand out shot glasses to Sophia and Chloe but Nova holds up her hands. "I'm breastfeeding."

"Drinking one standard alcoholic beverage a day at least two hours before breastfeeding is not known to be harmful to a baby."

Nova snatches the shot glass from me. "Leave it to you to fact my excuse away."

I hand a glass to Maya but she holds up her hand. "I'm trying to get pregnant."

"Just accept the glass. Paisley is going to fact your excuse away anyway," Nova mutters.

"Maybe I want to hear the fact," Maya says.

I oblige. "If you are trying for a baby, it is best to limit alcohol consumption to four drinks total per week. Since you haven't been drinking at all, this one shot will not hurt your chance to conceive."

I hand her a glass before pouring a shot of *Buccaneer's Whiskey* in each glass. "Raise your glasses. Here's to the bootleggers. Masters of sneaky snips and secret stashes. Thanks for keeping the party alive!"

"Bootleggers!" they shout in return before downing their shots.

"Wow." Nova rubs a hand over her chest. "I forgot how whiskey can burn."

Chloe smacks her lips. "But it's a good burn."

I gather the glasses and place them in my bag with the whiskey. Usually, we play a drinking game while we work our way through the nine holes of miniature golf but considering Nova's breastfeeding, Maya's trying to get pregnant, and Chloe's trying to get pregnant but doesn't want anyone to know, I didn't bother bringing any beer with me.

"Time to kick some mermaid ass!" Chloe shouts.

"Mermaids don't exist," I say because I enjoy ruffling Chloe. It's almost ridiculous how easy it is.

She glares at me. "Mermaids do exist."

Sophia threads her arm through Chloe's and nudges her toward the office. "Come on. Let's play some mini golf."

Cindy, the teenaged girl working in the office, groans when we arrive. "I thought you'd given up on mini golf. And now I'm going to have to kick you out."

Chloe scowls. "We've never been kicked out."

"But we have been politely asked to leave before," I add.

Chloe holds up a hand. "Not the same thing."

"Never said it was."

"What if I politely ask you to leave now?" Cindy asks.

"We'd decline and tell all the smugglers you have a crush on the captain of the football team," Sophia says.

Cindy rears back. "The captain of the football team is my best friend's boyfriend. She'd kill me."

Sophia hands her a wad of cash. "Give us our putters and scorecard and we'll be on our way."

Cindy groans. "I'm never working on Thursday again."

Once we have our putters and Maya has the scorecard – she's the only one trusted to keep score without cheating – we proceed to the first hole. Chloe skips to the tee.

"Anyone else tired of Chloe going first each time just because her name starts with a C?" Sophia asks. Nova and Maya raise their hands. I join them. I don't care who's first but I do enjoy teasing Chloe.

Chloe glares at Sophia. "What do you suggest?"

"Reverse alphabetical order."

"But you'd be first every time."

Sophia grins. "Exactly."

"We can pick names out of a hat," Maya suggests.

Chloe throws her arms wide. "And who's got a hat with them?"

I jiggle my phone at her. "I'll use a random name generator app."

She throws her putter on the ground. "This is some bullshit."

"Why? Because you're losing."

She narrows her eyes on me. "You hate to lose as much as I do."

It's true. I'm quite competitive. It's why I owned my own putter after all. I quickly input our names into the app.

"Sophia, you're first. Next are Maya, Nova, and Chloe. I'm last."

"Ha! Ha! You're last," Chloe taunts.

I ignore her. Being last has its advantages after all.

When we reach halfway, Maya collapses on the grass next to the mermaid at the ninth hole. "I can't believe I'm saying this but mini golf is harder sober."

The rest of us join her on the ground and form a circle. I wave the bottle of whiskey at her. "You want another shot?"

"Give it to me." Chloe snatches the bottle from me, unscrews the top, and drinks straight from the bottle. "Anyone else?"

"Might as well," Sophia says. Once she's had a drink, she hands the bottle to Maya who takes a dainty sip. She passes the bottle to Nova who gives me the bottle without drinking.

Chloe falls back to lay on the grass. "Who would have thought when we were playing mini golf last summer that this summer we'd all be in relationships?"

"Not every one of us is in a relationship," Nova says. "Paisley's still single."

Chloe waves her hand in the air. "It's only a matter of time before Paisley and Eli are knocking boots."

I growl. "Eli and I will not be knocking boots."

"Oh right. Because you hate him."

I blow out a breath. I may have been wrong on my assessment of Eli as an asshole. He hasn't been a jerk once since I've been brewing at the distillery.

On the contrary, he brings me coffee every morning. Mostly purchased from *Pirates Pastries* since he's now afraid of the coffee machine. And he checks on me periodically throughout the day to ensure I'm not working too hard.

In other words, he's been a gentleman. It's possible I was a bitch to him without reason. Or rather, the reason did not justify my rancor.

"Speaking of Eli." Sophia smirks.

I glance over my shoulder. What is he doing here? I scan the area and notice his brothers goofing off at the first hole.

"Hey, Eli!" Chloe waves him over. And I debate hitting her with my putter. Not in the head. But in the back of the knees wouldn't be so bad. Too bad she's laying on the grass.

Eli strolls toward us with a grin on his face and a sparkle in his stunning blue eyes. I could drown in those eyes.

"Settle a debate for us," Sophia says when he reaches us.

"What debate?"

"Do you think Paisley is cuter with or without her glasses?"

At the mention of my glasses, I slide them up my nose. "We weren't discussing my glasses."

Eli feigns studying me. "She's cute either way but with the glasses she's got the whole nerdy thing going on."

I scowl. "Nerdy thing?"

"You know mad scientist ready to overtake the world."

"Mad scientist?"

Chloe giggles. "We always did claim our little nerd would conquer the world."

"I'm not a nerd," I grumble.

"Too bad because the glasses sell the whole nerd look, Mr. Magoo," Eli says and I see red.

I jump to my feet and fist my hands on my hips. "Who do you think you are? Making fun of someone with glasses."

He holds up his hands and backs away. "I didn't mean…"

"I didn't mean," I mimic. "I am so tired of people saying they didn't mean anything when they call me a nerd or make fun of my glasses. I need glasses to see. What's funny about being visually impaired? Nothing I tell you."

I stomp away.

"I'm sorry," Eli shouts after me.

I ignore him. I was wrong. Eli is an asshole.

Chapter 14

"Lesson learned. Never piss anyone off who knows how to use a chemistry set." ~ Eli

ELI

I frown when I notice Paisley's office light on as I park at *Buccaneer's Whiskey*. I want to go to her. Explain I wasn't making fun of her. I was teasing her. It was meant to be light-hearted and fun. Plus, she's adorable when she's flustered. I didn't realize her wearing glasses was a trigger for her.

With a sigh, I exit my car and walk to the entrance. I won't be bringing Paisley a coffee this morning. I should probably ask my mom the best way a man can apologize. She'll know. She recently remarried and her new husband screwed things up left and right before he finally figured it out.

I unlock the doors to the building and make my way to my office; switching on lights as I go. I set my briefcase down before shrugging out of my suit jacket. Paisley's right. It's entirely too hot to wear a suit this time of year, but I have a conference call with some potential investors in *Apparoo* today.

I settle behind my desk and switch on my computer. While I wait for it to warm up, I open my drawer to get my agenda. But when I pull on the drawer, it doesn't move. I pull harder but it still doesn't budge. I grunt before yanking on it.

There's a click and a hiss before the drawer flies open and a cloud of red smoke appears. I cough as I wave the cloud away.

I jump to my feet when I notice the 'cloud' is now staining my fingers red. "What the hell?" I glance down at my suit. It now resembles a Jackson Pollock painting with splatters of paint on it.

I rip off my vest but the damage is already done. My vest and pants are covered in red.

Someone claps from the doorway. "This worked out better than I envisioned," Paisley says before pivoting away.

I chase after her. "What the hell, Paisley? You ruined my suit."

She rolls her eyes. "Don't be so melodramatic. It'll wash out."

"I have an investor meeting today."

She stills. "There was nothing on your agenda about an investor meeting."

"Because it doesn't involve the distillery."

"Whatever." She waves away my concerns. "You can wear your spare suit."

"Thank god I keep a spare suit in my closet."

She freezes. "In your closet?"

I moan. "What the hell did you do to my closet?"

"Nothing if you don't open it."

I run a hand down my face. "What did I do to deserve this treatment?"

She rears back. "You seriously have to ask?"

No, I don't. I know she's referring to the evening at mini golf.

"I was teasing, Paisley. You do know the word, don't you? You're supposed to be some genius. Your vocabulary should include the word 'teasing'."

She stabs my chest with her finger. "I know exactly what teasing means. I also know what bullying means. And the line between the two can be blurred especially when a person hits on a particular trigger."

"What's the issue with you and glasses? Tons of people wear glasses. It's not a big deal."

Pain flashes in those hazel eyes and I flinch. I didn't mean to hurt Paisley. I don't want her to ever feel pain.

"It just is a big deal." She spins on her heel and starts to stomp away but I shackle her wrist to stop her.

"Please tell me, Lace. I don't want to accidentally hurt you again." I nod to my red-stained pants. "Dry cleaning is too expensive."

She snorts. "As if you'll even notice an expense such as dry cleaning."

I rub my thumb over the pulse in her wrist and it spikes. I use it to my advantage. "Please, Lace. I promise I can keep a secret."

"It's not a secret, but I prefer not to discuss it."

"I understand. After today, we'll never discuss it again if you don't want to." Assuming I can persuade her to speak to me again. She hasn't spoken a word to me in the week since the incident at the Mermaid Mini Golf course.

She nibbles on her bottom lip as she contemplates her answer. My blood heats as I imagine being the one nibbling on her lip. Tasting those pretty pink lips. Tasting her. I bet she tastes better than the smoothest *Buccaneer Whiskey.*

"Fine. I'll tell you." She scans the area. "But not while we're standing in the hallway."

I try to steer her toward my office but she plants her feet. I change direction and lead her to her office instead. She locks the door behind us but when she tries to round her desk to sit behind it, I maneuver her to the sofa. This isn't about work. We're going to face each other and be comfortable during this discussion.

And I don't want her far away from me when I know she's hurting. If she'd let me, I'd wrap my arms around her and shield her from the world. She'd probably slap me for the thought alone. Paisley doesn't want anyone shielding her.

She fidgets with the hem of her t-shirt and I let her. I won't push her. Any more than I already have.

"I have two stepsisters," she blurts out.

When she doesn't continue, I ask, "Did you grow up with them?"

She nods. How did she grow up with sisters on Smuggler's Hideaway and I didn't know about them? The island isn't very big.

She must notice my confusion because she explains. "They're eight and nine years older than me."

The age difference explains it somewhat. But not completely.

"And have a different last name."

Ah. Now things are beginning to make sense. "Your dad remarried?"

"No." She blows out a breath. "My dad died when I was a baby. I don't remember him at all."

I can't resist touching her. It's the least I can do when she's in pain. I squeeze her hand and she clings to mine. Don't worry, Paisley. I won't let you go.

"Your mom remarried," I prod.

"Yes." She swallows. "I was five when Darcy and Regan came to live with us."

I make a mental note to find out where they are now. "What's their last name?"

Her brow wrinkles. "Thatcher. Why?"

Because it's easier to find people when you know their last name. "Why don't you have the same last name?" I ask instead.

"My stepfather never adopted me."

"Was your mom against the adoption?"

She shrugs. "Initially, she wanted me to be older when he adopted me."

She's not telling me the entire story. "But he never adopted you?"

"My stepfather and I never got along."

"Why not? Is he an asshole?"

"An asshole? What makes you think he's an asshole?"

I squeeze her hand. "I've known you since kindergarten. You were an adorable child. Any man would be proud for you to call him dad."

"Adorable?" She fiddles with her glasses. "I'm a nerd, remember?"

"I apologize. I was teasing. But now I realize I should have never called you a nerd or made fun of your glasses. I can assure you it will never happen again."

She studies my face and I drop all my guards. I let her see everything. How sincere I'm being. How much I admire her. How much I don't consider her my enemy.

"Okay. I accept your apology."

"Did your stepfather not want to adopt you because you wore glasses?" I ask since she still hasn't explained why her glasses are a trigger for her.

"Not exactly." She toys with a loose thread on her jeans. "To be more accurate, the glasses were more of a symbol of why he didn't approve of me."

"Approve of you? What kind of bullshit is this? Parents don't approve or disapprove of their children. They're children. You love them and support them."

"Ha!" She barks out a laugh but she's not amused. "My stepdad wouldn't know what love and support is when it comes to me. Darcy and Regan are a different matter. They're beautiful and perfect. Never mind how Darcy had braces for three years and Regan had a nose job. They're beautiful and beauty is all that matters."

"Beauty is in the eye of the beholder."

"The judges of the Miss Maryland contest think otherwise."

"Miss Maryland? As in a beauty contest?"

She nods. "Yep. It's how Chloe and I became such close friends. Her mom forced her to compete in beauty contests all the time." She gasps. "Please don't say anything to Chloe. She doesn't want anyone to know about her past."

I pat her thigh. "I won't say anything." I blow out a breath. "I have to admit I'm still confused. I don't understand what your stepsisters competing in beauty contests has to do with glasses."

"My stepdad believes beauty is everything. Women don't need brains because they should be in the kitchen cooking anyway. But they should be pretty to catch a husband."

I growl. "You have got to be kidding me."

"I wish," she mumbles. "My stepdad pushed and cajoled my mom until she agreed I'd compete in the beauty contests, too. But I wasn't allowed to compete with my glasses on. The first time I went on stage I tripped on a step I didn't see and ended up sprawled across the floor. My stepdad was humiliated. And it was all the fault of my glasses."

"Darcy and Regan nearly peed themselves laughing and I never heard the end of it. Seriously. We can't have a conversation without them bringing it up. They think it's hilarious."

I frown. "What about your mom? Didn't she stop them?"

She glances away but not before I notice the pain in her eyes. "My stepdad bullies my mom. She thinks she loves him but really she's just afraid to be on her own."

Which explains why Paisley has an independent streak a mile wide.

I pinch her chin and force her to meet my gaze. "I'm sorry, Lace. I'm sorry for everything. I'm sorry your family are a bunch of assholes. I'm sorry your mom didn't protect you. I'm sorry I teased you about your glasses. I'm just plain sorry."

"I already forgave you. There's no need to do a big apology."

She's joking but the pain in her hazel eyes is breaking my heart. I can't stand the sight of her pain. I do the only thing I can think of.

I meld my lips to hers.

Chapter 15

"Hell, yeah." ~ Eli's only thought

ELI

Paisley's lips are as soft as they look. I trace her lips with my tongue.

"Let me in, Lace."

She sighs before opening. I sink into her mouth. She tastes of coffee and sweetness with a bite of the exotic. And I can't get enough of it. I palm her neck as I explore her. I want to memorize every inch, every crevice.

She grasps my biceps and melts into me. She isn't a silent participant, though. Not my Paisley. Her tongue searches for mine and we duel for supremacy.

I growl and tighten my hold on her neck. I love how independent she is but in the bedroom, I'm in charge.

She doesn't relent. Of course not. I lift her up and place her on my lap. Where she belongs.

I drag her forward until her core is pressed against my hardness. She startles before pushing away from me. "We shouldn't be doing this."

Her lips are swollen from my kisses, strands of her hair have escaped her ponytail, and her glasses are askew. She's never been more beautiful.

I tuck a strand of hair behind her ear. "Why not?"

"Why not? Are you deliberately being obtuse?"

She pushes against me, but I don't let her go. If I give her any space, she'll flee. Not happening.

"Stay with me. Why am I being obtuse?"

She leans as far away from me as possible while still sitting in my lap and crosses her arms over her chest. "You're going to pretend you want me?"

I lift my hips to press my hard length against her. "Biology doesn't lie."

She scowls at me. "There's a difference between you physically wanting me and you emotionally wanting me."

I nod. "Okay. Let me clear up any confusion. I want you, Paisley."

She rolls her eyes. "Don't lie to get laid. It's beneath you."

"I'm not lying. I want you." She snorts. "Why don't you believe me?"

She stares at me for a long moment and I can practically see the wheels turning in her mind. After a while, she shakes her head. "No."

I finally have her where I want her. I'm not letting her retreat. I palm her face. "Please, Lace. Tell me why you hate me."

"I don't hate you."

"Liar." I kiss her nose. "If you don't tell me, I can't convince you you're wrong."

"You can't convince me I'm wrong anyway."

This is my chance. "Prove it." Paisley loves to prove things. And she can't resist a challenge.

"I can't believe you don't remember." She huffs.

I squeeze her hips. "Don't remember what?"

"Our date."

She glares at me and I search my memory but I come up blank. "Our date?"

Her nostrils flare. "This is what I mean. You don't remember."

How can I not remember a date with Paisley? "Remind me, please."

"I asked you to the movies. You said yes. You never showed up. End of story."

It's obviously not the end of the story or she wouldn't have spent the past decade hating me. "How can I not…" I trail off when a glimpse of a memory hits me. "Wait. Was this our first semester senior year?"

She nods.

"I remember we agreed to go to the movies. But I didn't go because I had to work. I got an extra shift last minute at the amusement park. I texted you."

Her lips purse. "Obviously not."

I scour my memory. "Oh shit. I forgot. My phone died and the message didn't go through."

"I stood near the concession stand waiting for you for an hour. My evil stepsisters thought it was hilarious. They still haven't stopped teasing me about it."

I palm her face. "I'm sorry, Paisley. I didn't realize the message hadn't gone through until the next day. When I approached you at school to explain, you brushed me off. I thought it wasn't a big deal to you."

"What did you expect me to do? Cry and rant in front of the entire student population?"

"Instead, you pretended it didn't matter. Acted like our friendship meant nothing to you."

"And you dubbed me Paisley the Perpetual Know It All."

I cringe. "I never should have called you that name. I was hurt and lashing out. I'm sorry. And I'm sorry I didn't show up for our date. When I realized the message hadn't gone through, I should have insisted on explaining myself to you. I was afraid you didn't care."

"And then you forgot all about it."

I squeeze her neck. "I forced it out of my mind since I didn't want to know the girl I had a crush on didn't care enough about me to get mad I ghosted her. Will you forgive me for being an asshole?"

She sighs. "I don't want to forgive you but you've proven you're not an asshole. You offered me this space for the brewery, you bring me coffee every morning. I just wish you'd told me you had to work the night of our date."

"I should have, but I'm a fucking idiot."

"Don't expect me to disagree."

I bark out a laugh.

"I wasn't joking."

"Nope." I kiss her nose.

She squirms and I grasp her hips. "Don't move."

"I want to get up."

"My cock doesn't understand the difference."

She freezes. "Your cock?"

I capture her hand and lay it on my hard length. Her eyes flare. "You're still excited?"

"Lace, you're sitting on my lap. Naturally, I'm excited."

"But we were having a serious conversation."

"The only words my cock understands are yes, harder, and don't stop."

She licks her lips as she stares at my crotch. "Interesting. I wonder if there are other words it understands. Maybe keep going, just like that."

I groan. "You're not helping things."

"Your cock twitched. I think I'm helping."

"I'm trying to be a gentleman here."

Her nose wrinkles. "Why? You were ready to ravage me before when I thought you hated me."

"I never hated you."

"Yes. I realize this now. Which is why I'm interested in your cock."

"You have to stop saying cock. He'll never calm down if you don't."

"Who said I want it to calm down?"

"Lace," I growl. "Stop teasing me."

She bats her eyelashes. "Or what?"

"You're going to get fucked right here on this sofa."

"Promises. Pro—"

I don't let her finish. I smash my lips to hers while wrapping an arm around her waist to pull her near. I moan when her core lands on top of my hard length. My cock weeps in happiness.

I wrench my lips from hers and smatter kisses along her jaw until I reach her ear. "If you don't want this, tell me."

She grinds herself on my hardness. "I want this."

I bite her earlobe in punishment. "You're a little tease."

"It's not teasing if I put out."

My cock twitches again. It doesn't understand why I keep talking. Why I haven't buried myself in Paisley's wet heat yet. I don't have an answer since I can't remember why we aren't naked and fucking either.

I squeeze Paisley's hips. "Remove your pants."

She doesn't hesitate. She stands and kicks off her shoes before shoving her jeans and panties down her legs.

I expected her to blush or stumble or be shy in some way, but she's not. My independent woman isn't embarrassed or shy about sex. It's fucking addicting.

"Do you have a condom or shall I get one?"

I frown. "You have condoms?"

"It's important to be prepared for all eventualities."

I love it when my nerdy girl comes out to play. "Grab a condom. I don't have my wallet with me."

She saunters to her desk and I watch her ass as it jiggles while she walks. I can't wait to bend her over the sofa and sink into her while staring at those perfect globes. I wonder if she'd let me spank her.

"Are you going to undress?" she asks as she walks toward me. "Or would you prefer if I strip you?"

The vision of Paisley removing my clothes is appealing but I can't wait to get inside her. I've waited more than a decade. I'm done waiting.

I unzip my slacks before lifting my ass to pull the material down to my thighs. My cock juts out and aims straight for Paisley. It knows what it wants.

I snag the condom from her and roll it on before patting my thighs. "Hop on."

She lifts her t-shirt before climbing onto my lap. She straddles my thighs on her knees. I draw my hands up her inner thighs – the skin is as smooth as I'd imagined – until I reach her core. I part her lips to find her clit.

I rub circles around it until she digs her fingers into my shoulders. Damn. I should have removed my shirt. I want to feel her hands on my naked skin.

Next time.

And there will be a next time. No way am I letting this be a one and done situation. Not since I've realized Paisley doesn't hate me.

"Do you want more?"

"Obviously. I'm naked and poised above you and you're wearing a condom."

I chuckle. I should have known she'd take my question literally. I can be literal, too.

"Do you want me to sink my fingers into your pussy?"

"Yes."

I tease her opening with one finger. I can feel how wet she is. For me. She's wet for me. The thought has my chest warming and my cock weeping.

"Inside," she orders.

"You're not in charge here."

"I am on top."

"I can top from the bottom."

She opens her mouth but I don't let her speak. I thrust two fingers into her pussy and her walls flutter around me. She's tight and warm and wet. My cock is jealous of my fingers as I plunge in and out of her.

"Ride my fingers. Get yourself off."

She grinds herself on my fingers and I press the heel of my palm against her clit. She moans and I do it again.

"Do you like the feel of my fingers inside of you?"

"Do. You. Need. To. Ask?" she stutters.

No, but I do enjoy the feel of her walls tightening whenever I talk dirty to her. Who would have thought my nerdy girl enjoyed dirty talk? I want to learn all there is to know about Paisley. There's much more to her than a smart girl who wears glasses.

Speaking of glasses. I remove hers and throw them on the coffee table.

"What are you doing?"

"There's no need for glasses when I'm going to make you blind with passion."

Her eyes flare. "Okay."

"I need you to come for me, Lace. My cock wants in that pussy. I want to feel you squeezing my cock the way you're squeezing my fingers now."

I quicken my pace and Paisley bounces on my fingers. I add a third finger and her walls flutter.

"Come, Paisley. Come all over my hand."

"Yes," she moans as her climax hits her. I continue to glide in and out of her until it wanes.

I remove my fingers and position her over me.

"Now, it's my turn."

I notch my cock at her entrance. I start to lift up but Paisley impales herself on me.

"Fuck, Paisley," I moan at the feel of her surrounding me.

"Fucking is precisely what we are doing."

I chuckle even as my cock hardens further at her words. I've never been this turned on and amused at the same time.

Only Paisley can do this to me.

Chapter 16

"And people claim I'm the stubborn one. They obviously haven't met Eli." ~ Paisley

PAISLEY

I slump into Eli and he wraps his arms around me. I'm completely sated.

Usually, I need more time to orgasm. And I definitely don't ever orgasm twice in one session. But not with Eli. He touches me and every nerve ending in my body comes alive.

Eli brushes his fingers through my hair. My ponytail didn't survive. My hair is probably sticking up in all directions. For the first time in my life, I don't care how my hair looks. No one's here to see it.

Besides Eli. I should probably extract myself from him. The desire to burrow myself into his chest is strong. But I don't want to give him the wrong idea. I count to five before pushing away and standing.

"We should get back to work. I need to check on several items."

Eli frowns. "Are you trying to put distance between us?"

Obviously. Sex is sex. But feelings are different. I know myself well enough to realize I could very easily become attached to Eli. I don't want to have my heart broken again. Once was enough for me.

I snatch my jeans and panties from the floor and sit on the coffee table to put them on. I scowl. My thighs are covered in red dye.

Eli laughs. "Your prank came back to bite you on the ass."

I glare at him. "Never mind. The dye isn't permanent."

He stands and pulls up his pants and buttons them. "Come on." He holds out his hand to me. "You can wash off in my private bathroom."

I will not be the one opening the door to his private bathroom.

He drops his hand. "What did you do to my bathroom?"

"Nothing. As long as you don't open the door."

"So, basically, I can never open my closet or bathroom door again?"

"Pretty much."

"I've learned my lesson. Never piss you off."

"Good."

"If you can't use my bathroom, you can use the ladies room."

I'm shaking my head before he can finish. "I'm not traipsing through the building with sex hair."

He smirks. "I happen to like your sex hair."

I roll my eyes. "You would. You're a male. You're reveling in our sexual encounter."

"Not any sexual encounter. A sexual encounter with you."

I ignore the implication. "I'll drive home and clean up. I shouldn't be long."

I start toward my desk to grab my keys but Eli stops me. "I'll drive you."

"No thank you. I'm perfectly capable of driving myself."

"My house is closer than yours. We'll be there and back faster than if you drive to your house."

"This is Smuggler's Hideaway. Nothing is far."

His eyes narrow on me. "Are you afraid of being seen with me?"

I wish I could lie and say I'm not. But I'm not one for lying. Lying causes miscommunication and there's been enough miscommunication between the two of us.

"I prefer not to be seen with you in this condition. People will conclude we've had sex and before you know it everyone on the island – especially my friends – will be hounding us to begin a relationship."

He scowls. "And you don't want to be in a relationship with me?"

I wave a hand in dismissal. "I'm fine on my own."

"I apologized for what I did in high school. I was a dumbass. Please don't hold my idiocy against me."

"I'm not. If anything, I should apologize to you for being a bitch. I should have confronted you and asked you why you didn't show up. Instead, I assumed you stood me up."

He steps closer. "You're not a bitch."

"I'm not but I did act bitchy toward you. I'm sorry."

"There's no need to apologize."

"Nonetheless. My apology has been said."

"Thank you. Can we now get going? I need to be back for an investor meeting in an hour."

"You go ahead. There's no need for us to go together."

"I thought you were going to stop holding what I did in high school against me."

"I'm not holding it against you." I'm also not planning on getting involved with Eli. I had a weak moment and we had sex. Nothing more. Nothing less.

He blows out a breath before sitting on the sofa.

"What are you doing? You have an investor meeting to attend."

"I'm not going anywhere until you tell me what this is about."

I fist my hands on my hips. "What right do you have to demand answers from me?"

He unfurls from the sofa and prowls toward me. I am not his prey. I refuse to move. I will hold my ground.

He crowds me until I can feel his heat, smell his scent. I shove my hands in my pockets before I reach for him and demand a second round. There will be no second rounds with Eli.

I have nothing against casual sex. But sex with him is anything but emotionless. I can't afford to go down that road. It ends in heartbreak.

"I've been inside you. I've felt you come on my cock and on my fingers. I plan to do it again, Lace."

"Lace?" I grab the chance to derail the conversation. "My name is Paisley. Not Lace."

He skims a finger down my arm. I lock my muscles but I can't help the goosebumps from forming at his touch.

"To everyone else, you're Paisley. To me, you're Lace. A beautiful, intricate, and complicated pattern."

"I'm not beautiful."

"You are. But I'm not letting you change the topic." I open my mouth to snark at him but he places a finger on my lips. "And you know exactly what topic I'm referring to. Why won't you give this – us – a chance?"

"You never asked for a chance."

"You're right. I didn't. My apologies. Lace, will you give this relationship a chance?"

I don't hesitate. "No, thank you."

He rears back. "What? Why not?"

"Do I have to give reasons?"

"Yes, you do." He nods. "It's obvious you want me. You light up whenever I touch you. Your pulse is beating erratically at how near I am now."

I raise my foot intent on stepping back. Hold on. I don't retreat. I don't give up. I set my foot back down.

"My body may want you but good sex isn't a foundation to begin a relationship."

"Good sex," he grumbles. "We had phenomenal sex."

"Whatever. Sex isn't a foundation."

"Forget the sex."

I wish I could but I won't forget our little foray on the sofa for a long time. I'll probably dream of it every night for years to come.

"Sex is off the table."

I raise an eyebrow. "Sex is off the table?"

"Trust me. I don't want sex off of the table. But if abstaining will convince you to give us a try, I'm willing to abstain."

Damn it. He's pushing me into a corner. I don't want to tell him why I'm not interested in a relationship but I have no choice. I recognize a man who won't give up.

"There's more to the story."

"Of course, there is. My Paisley is complicated." He grasps my hand and leads me to the sofa.

"I'm not your Paisley."

"Not yet." He winks. "First, I have to dispel whatever bullshit is up here." He taps my temple.

"It's not bullshit."

"Prove it."

"I will."

He motions for me to proceed. "I'm listening."

"I had a serious relationship in college with Ryan."

He growls and I glare. "Sorry. I'll be quiet."

"I thought we would get married. But he dumped me senior year."

He squeezes my thigh. "I'm sorry. Getting your heart broken is no fun. But it's no reason to hide away and never get involved in a relationship again."

"There's more." I inhale a deep breath before confessing the rest of the story. "He got engaged to Darcy the next week. They're married now and have two children."

He growls. "Darcy? Your stepsister?" I nod. "Your stepsister was fooling around with your boyfriend?"

"He visited me during the summer break and met Darcy. Apparently, they fell in love at first sight."

"Ryan should have broken up with you then. Not continued to lead you on."

I swallow. "He should have. But being cheated on isn't the worst of the story."

He blows out a breath. "I'm afraid to ask."

"Then, don't ask." I try to stand but he squeezes my hip to stop me.

"What is the worst part of the story, Lace?"

"He's also part of the whole let's make fun of Paisley thing my family does."

"Asshole," he mutters.

"I overheard him telling Darcy he was never attracted to me. He could never be attracted to a woman who wears glasses."

"You should probably stop eavesdropping on people."

I slap his shoulder. "I can't help it if I always happen to be in the right place at the right time."

"I'd argue you are in the wrong place at the wrong time."

"Of course, you would. You love to argue."

"Only with you, Lace. Only with you."

"You argue with your brothers all the time."

He groans. "My brothers are the bane of my existence."

"And yet you built this company for them so you can spend time with them."

"I'm sorry, Lace. I wish you had the family you deserve but your family being a den of assholes doesn't mean you should avoid relationships."

I disagree. I've tried enough relationships in my thirty years. I have my friends. I'm perfectly happy to spend the rest of my life being the fun aunt.

My heart clenches at the thought of always being alone. Attending every event by myself. Never having a partner who understands me.

Fine. I'm lying to myself. I'm not perfectly happy being alone. But I don't want to have my heart broken either.

"I'm not interested in a relationship."

Eli smirks. "I'll change your mind."

"You can try."

"And I'll succeed." His phone rings and he swears under his breath. He digs it out and reads the display. "I need to answer this but this discussion isn't over."

"You can't have a discussion by yourself."

He kisses my nose. "Which is why we'll be having the discussion together." He opens the door and saunters away.

I glare at his backside as he hurries down the hallway. He reaches the door to the offices and glances over his shoulder at me. He winks before disappearing.

Eli thinks he's won this round. He has no idea how stubborn I can be.

Chapter 17

ELI

Paisley opens the door and scowls at me. "What are you doing here?"

I let my gaze linger over her, taking in every detail. She's wearing an emerald green dress that clings to her figure, the neckline dipping just enough to reveal a hint of cleavage. The skirt splits high on one side, stretching well past her knee, promising to reveal her bare legs with each step she takes.

My Lace is cute in her jeans and t-shirts but in this dress? She's sexy as fuck.

"You look gorgeous."

Her cheeks darken and I watch as the blush travels down her neck to her chest. I want to follow the path with my tongue. My cock hardens and lengthens as I imagine drawing those spaghetti straps off her shoulders to reveal her chest.

"You didn't answer my question. What are you doing here?"

She taps her foot and I notice she's wearing a pair of matching emerald green stilettos. Damn, how I'd love to sink into her while she's wearing nothing but those shoes.

Paisley snaps her fingers in front of my face. "Earth to Eli. What are you doing here?"

I force my thoughts away from bending Paisley over the couch and grin. "I'm your date for the evening."

She purses her lips. I know those pretty pink lips taste sweet with a hint of the exotic. Just like Paisley. She's sweet but she's also unconventional. I will never get bored of this woman.

"Date? I never agreed to go on a date with you."

I feign confusion. "You didn't?"

She narrows her eyes on me. "You know how I feel about miscommunication regarding dates."

Damn. I didn't think. "I'm sorry."

She sighs. "It's fine. I shouldn't have brought it up. It was bitchy of me."

I grasp her hand. "You're not a bitch."

"It's nice of you to lie."

I didn't lie but we don't have time to debate this. "We need to be going."

She waves away my concern. "There's no reason to worry about being on time. This is Smuggler's Hideaway. No one will be on time for the dress rehearsal for the end of the summer ball."

I clear my throat. "Actually, there is no dress rehearsal."

"I should have known my friends were lying to me. We've never had a dress rehearsal before. Why now? This is what I get for skipping those committee meetings."

She steps back and reaches for the doorknob. I stand in the doorframe before she can shut me out.

"Don't make me go to this event without a date. The vultures will be out."

"What event? You admitted there's no dress rehearsal less than a minute ago or did you forget?"

I ignore her taunt. "The event is a fundraiser to raise money for women's rights."

"A fundraiser? On Smuggler's Hideaway?"

I tug on my bowtie. "Not exactly."

She crosses her arms over her chest, pushing her breasts together, and I nearly say fuck it. Screw the fundraiser. There are more exciting things I'd rather be doing.

But I promised Paisley I'd show her there's more to us than our chemistry. I can't fail at the first hurdle.

"Explain yourself before I shut this door in your face."

"The fundraiser is in D.C."

"D.C. It's already six o'clock. How are we going to drive to D.C. in time for this event?"

"We won't be driving."

"How else…" She trails off with a shake of her head. "You have a plane."

And she's clearly unimpressed. At least, I never have to worry if Paisley is with me for my money.

"It's not my plane per se."

She lifts her eyebrow.

"I share it with a few other people."

She snorts. "It's still your plane."

"If I agree it's my plane, will you accompany me to this event?"

"The event is to raise money for charities that support women's causes?" Paisley can't hide her interest. I know how important women's causes are to her. It's the reason why I accepted an invitation to the fundraiser.

"Yes. I have some brochures in my car." I motion to the vehicle waiting at the curb.

"Car? It's a limousine."

"You could pretend to be impressed by my wealth," I joke.

"The way you pretended the jet wasn't yours?"

I offer her my elbow. "Would you please accompany me to the fundraiser? Or are you scared?"

"I'm not scared to attend an event with you."

I lean forward and say the words I know will guarantee her attendance. "Prove it."

She snatches her purse from the table next to her and waves me toward the limo. "Let's go."

I cough to hide my amusement. Paisley is a complicated woman but she can't resist a dare. Never could. It's why she spent nearly as much time in detention in high school as Sophia and Chloe.

She marches toward the limo and I fall in line behind her. Sex may be off the table but I never said I wouldn't stare at her ass. And her ass in this silky dress is a thing of beauty. She turns toward the limo and the slit in her dress widens to allow me a glimpse of her bare leg.

My cock twitches. Shit. I can't get hard in this outfit. Tuxedo pants would telegraph my excitement to Paisley. I'd rather keep my horniness out of the conversation. For now.

I recite the quarterly figures for *Apparoo* until my cock gets the message. Once it calms down, I follow Paisley to the limo. The driver steps out but I wave him away.

"I've got this."

I open the door and usher Paisley inside. Goosebumps break out on her arm when I touch her elbow. I can't resist stroking my thumb against her skin. She shivers before yanking her arm away.

We settle in the back seat and the vehicle begins driving toward the private airfield across the bridge on the mainland.

Paisley caresses the leather seat as she scans the interior. "Do you own this limo as well?"

"No."

She raises an eyebrow.

"I rented it for tonight."

"I've never been in a limo before."

"Not even for prom?"

"High school kids don't ride in limos to prom on Smuggler's Hideaway. They use golf carts decorated like smugglers."

I chuckle. "I forgot. When Zane went to prom, he dressed up as a bootlegger. His date was not amused."

"Bootleggers can be quite dashing."

I narrow my eyes on her and feign irritation. "Do you think Zane is more handsome than me?"

"More handsome? You're presuming I find you handsome at all."

I grin. "You think I'm handsome. Paisley Bardot wouldn't let just any man into her pants."

She glances away. I notice her bare shoulders have a smattering of freckles on them. I want to trace them with my tongue. When it comes to Paisley, what part of her body don't I want to trace with my tongue?

"You don't know me as well as you think you do. Maybe I sleep around. Maybe I have one-night stands more often."

I growl at the idea of my Paisley letting anyone besides me into her body.

"I know you, Lace. I know you're the smartest person I've ever met."

She rolls her eyes. "You own a business with Jeremy Holland."

"I stand by my statement."

"Flattery will get you nowhere."

I chuckle. "I know. Because I know you."

"You didn't know I had two evil stepsisters until last week."

I hate how I didn't know how bad her family life was growing up. "You don't consider Darcy and Regan family. Your family consists of Sophia, Chloe, Nova, and Maya for whom you'd do anything."

"Don't be jealous I have better friends than you do."

"I'm not jealous." I hook my pinky with hers. When she doesn't snatch her hand away, I take it as a victory.

We cross the bridge onto the mainland and Paisley glances behind us to watch Smuggler's Island fade away.

"Are you nervous about being away from the island? I promise I'll have you back before your bedtime."

"I'm not nervous. Just curious where we're going."

"It's killing you to not whip out your phone and research where the nearest private airport is, isn't it?"

"It's in Jettson's Way."

I chuckle. "Is there anything you don't know?"

"It's impossible to know everything. I haven't spent any time studying Ancient Roman history or learning the Japanese language and my ability to program computers is limited."

I smile. "I wasn't being literal."

"It's important you don't put me up on a pedestal. I'm not a very good climber."

"What if I install an elevator in the pedestal?"

"It's good you realize how high this pedestal you're putting me on is." Her shoulders tremble with her laughter and I can't resist her skin. I lean forward to dot kisses along her shoulder to her collarbone. She shivers in response.

"Are you cold?" I tease.

"I didn't bring a shawl. I didn't realize we'd be traveling North."

I open the cupboard next to the bar and remove a wrapped package.

"What's this?" Paisley asks when I hand it to her.

"Open it and find out."

"Are you going to shower me with expensive gifts and fancy trips until I agree to date you?"

I waggle my eyebrows. "You're already on a date with me."

"It doesn't count since I didn't realize what was happening. But it would have been a waste to get all dressed up and not go anywhere."

I glance down at her outfit. "A damn shame if no one else had a chance to experience how beautiful you are tonight."

"You don't have to say I'm beautiful."

"But you are beautiful," I say before kissing her shoulder again. "Although, I will be jealous of every man who stares at you tonight."

"No men will stare at me."

"You really don't know how beautiful you are."

"Trust me. I have two evil stepsisters and a wicked stepfather who would disagree with you."

"They're assholes. Forget about them." I tap the package. "Now, open your present."

She places a finger underneath the tape, making sure to not tear the wrapping as she opens the gift.

I chuckle. "Why am I not surprised you don't rip into presents?"

"There's no reason to be a savage. I wasn't…" She trails off when she opens the box. She pulls the lace shawl out and lifts it in the air. "It's gorgeous."

"I know you don't care but it's made of leavers lace from France."

She caresses the lace with her fingers. "It's unbelievably soft."

"As is your beautiful skin." I trace a finger down her arm and she shivers in response.

"I'll accept this gift if you stop calling me beautiful."

I'll call her beautiful as often as I want to. Until she realizes how beautiful she is.

When we eventually part ways, she'll know just how beautiful a woman she is.

Chapter 18

PAISLEY

Eli wraps the lace shawl over my shoulders. "Are you ready?"

I glance out of the limo at the red carpet. There are people lined up on either side of it as well as reporters waiting at the curb.

"I didn't realize our arrival would be documented."

He kisses my nose. "Ignore them. This night is for you and me."

Not exactly. "And the money we raise for women's equality."

He smiles. "Naturally."

The driver knocks on the door. I don't get a chance to respond before he opens it. Eli steps out and offers me his hand. I let him help me out of the vehicle since the slit in this dress could be pornographic if I'm not careful.

Flashes from the numerous cameras nearly blind me as we walk from the limo down the red carpet to the entry of the Smithsonian Art Museum. A woman is waiting at the door.

"Good evening, Mr. Raider." She flashes him a brilliant smile before narrowing her eyes on me. "You didn't RSVP with a guest."

"Oh? Would you prefer we leave?"

She immediately backpedals. "Of course not."

A security guard opens the door and we enter the museum. It's already crowded with groups of people standing around drinking champagne. The area is adorned with floral arrangements and artistic centerpieces on various cocktail tables scattered throughout the room. The colors white, purple, and green feature prominently.

A woman bustles toward us. "Mr. Raider." Her gaze travels over his body and she bites her lip. I wouldn't be surprised if she ripped her clothes off and offered herself to him as a sacrifice.

My stomach sours with jealousy – this woman is gorgeous in the way my stepsisters are and I will never be. A growl escapes before I can stop it.

Eli glances at me and smiles in reassurance before placing a hand on my hip and squeezing. The move is possessive, which normally irks me – men shouldn't own women – but instead of being annoyed, my body fills with warmth at his claim on me.

The woman's eyes flick to Eli's hand and she scowls. She covers up the scowl quickly, though, and smiles sweetly at Eli. "Can we get a photograph of you in front of the sponsor wall?"

Eli frowns. "Must we?"

"It is an opportunity for sponsors to promote their brands."

"Do you mind?" he asks me.

"Of course not." I try to step away from him but he tightens his hold on me.

"I'm not going alone."

I don't have a chance to protest before he ushers me to the sponsor wall. My eyes widen when I realize *Apparoo* is one of the biggest sponsors.

A man rushes toward us. "Can I take your shawl?"

"Um…" He snatches it from me before I can ask who he is and why he wants my shawl.

He caresses the fabric. "I may steal this from you, gorgeous."

It was the first gift Eli ever gave me. It's way too expensive and I will probably never have another opportunity to wear it again. But I will cherish it, nonetheless. And no one will steal it from me.

"Don't worry, boo. I'm kidding." He winks and shuffles away.

I try to follow him but Eli stops me. "We still need to take the picture."

"I shouldn't be in the picture."

"Why not?"

"Because I'm no one."

He circles my waist and pulls me flush to him. "Lace, you aren't no one. You're the most gorgeous woman in the room. I couldn't be prouder to have you on my arm."

I should protest. He's wrong. I'm nowhere near the most gorgeous woman in the room. But I find myself melting into his arms instead.

He kisses my forehead and – flash! – a camera goes off. "Thank you," the photographer says. "This is the best picture of the night thus far."

I feel my cheeks warm. I forgot we were in the middle of getting our picture taken. I am usually a rational person but Eli can rattle my thoughts.

Eli escorts me away from the wall and the man with my shawl runs toward us. "Every woman in the room hates you." He giggles. "I think I love you." He hands me my shawl, kisses my cheek, and rushes away.

"Who was he?" I ask as I stare after him.

"Danny works for *Apparoo.* He helps with all of our charity endeavors."

"Endeavors?" I raise my eyebrows. "You sponsor more good causes?"

"I don't. This is my one good cause. Each member of the board has a charity they've chosen for the company to support."

A waitress passes by and Eli snatches two flutes of champagne from her. He hands me one and I sip on it. I grimace and he bursts into laughter.

"I'll get you a beer." He takes my glass and marches toward the bar I didn't notice set up in the corner. I chase after him.

"The champagne is fine." I try to steal my glass back from him.

He holds the glass in the air. Even with four-inch heels on, I can't reach it. "If you don't enjoy champagne, you don't have to drink it."

He whirls around and places the flutes on the bar. "Can we have two bottles of beer, please?"

The bartender frowns. "Beer? I don't…" He scans the available drinks.

His colleague notices him floundering. "We have some beer in the kitchen. I'll grab you two."

Eli settles at the bar to wait. "I can't believe you," I mutter to him.

"What? You want a beer, you get a beer. I don't understand what the big deal is."

I motion to the room full of elegant people wearing cocktail dresses and tuxedos while drinking champagne out of fancy glasses. "We'll stick out."

He grins down at me. "Lace, you already stick out."

I frown and he kisses my nose.

"Not because you don't fit in but because you're obviously special."

Now I roll my eyes. "Did you watch YouTube videos on how to be charming before tonight?"

He puffs up his chest. "You think I'm charming."

"I think you're over the top."

"I am who I am."

The bartender arrives and sets two glasses of beer down in front of Eli. Eli hands me one before picking his up.

"To many more evenings spent together," he says as he clinks his glass with mine.

I narrow my eyes on him. "Did you forget I don't want to get involved with you?"

He smirks. "And yet where are you this evening?"

"Because my friends tricked me."

He tweaks my nose. "As if anyone could trick Paisley Bardot." He offers me his elbow. "Shall we have a peek at the items up for auction?"

I'm curious what type of items could interest the rich and thread my arm through his. He leads me toward the display of auction items.

The first item is a necklace. "This jade necklace would match your dress."

I notice the starting bid is five thousand dollars. I drag Eli away. "You are not bidding on a five thousand dollar necklace for me."

"But I want to spoil you."

"Spoil me by buying me a new beer fermentation tank."

"Send Dakota the specifics and she'll order it."

I screech to a halt. "Eli Raider, you will not buy me brewery equipment."

"You just said I could spoil you by buying you a fermentation tank."

I huff. "I was joking."

He tugs on my arm. "We'll find something else you want."

I refuse to move. "Why don't we mingle instead?"

He barks out a laugh. "Mingle? You, Paisley Bardot, are going to mingle?"

I narrow my eyes on him. "I can mingle. I'm not socially awkward."

"Nope. You just find most people boring." He leans close to whisper in my ear, "Rich people tend to be extremely boring."

"What are the two of you whispering about?" a woman asks as she stops in front of us.

"What I can buy to spoil her," Eli answers.

"And, as I've explained to him several times, I don't want him to spoil me."

The woman bats her eyelashes at Eli. "You can spoil me as much as you want."

"Sorry. I'm a one-woman man." He squeezes my arm. "And this is the one woman."

"How utterly boring," she says and glides away.

I'm confused. "Being monogamous is boring?"

"Who knows what she meant?" He motions to the other auction items. "Shall we continue?"

"Only if you promise not to bid on anything for me."

"What if I accidentally bid on an item for you?"

"How do you accidentally bid on an item? Oops. My pen slipped and my wallet opened and now it's ten thousand dollars lighter?"

He grins. "It could happen."

"You're delusional." I shake my head as I sip on my beer.

"I'm…" He trails off when he notices a woman making a beeline for us. "I apologize in advance," he whispers.

"Apologize? What for? Do you have gas?"

He barks out a laugh as the woman reaches us.

"Is it true?" she demands.

"Lucinda, it's lovely to see you." Based on the way Eli's gritting his teeth, he's lying.

"Who is this?" She practically snarls at me. "Is it true the great Eli Raider is off the market?"

"The great Eli Raider? Who's he?"

I scan the room as if I'm searching for this mystical creature and Eli pinches me. "Behave."

I mutter Chloe's favorite line. "Why start now?"

Lucinda's nostrils flare as she glares at me. "Is this her?"

I offer her my hand. "Nice to meet you. I'm Paisley."

She looks down her nose at me. "And you're drinking a beer."

"I own a brewery."

The woman's lips purse as her gaze travels up and down my body. "Of course you do."

"Lucinda," Eli growls. "Be nice."

"Why?" She throws her arms in the air. "I've waited years for you to realize who I am to you and you settle for this… this… this thing."

I'm confused. Is Eli in a relationship with this woman? Why did he have sex with me then? Why is he chasing me?

"Can someone give me the Cliff Notes version on what's happening now?"

Eli sighs. "Lucinda and I have known each other from college."

"We dated. We were a couple for years," Lucinda says.

"No, we weren't. You were my plus one whenever I had to attend one of these events."

"You took me home."

I do not want to hear this. I know Eli's been with other women. Obviously. He's thirty and a billionaire. Plus, he's handsome. He could have a harem if he wanted to. But I do not want to know the details. I refuse to let the jealousy building in my stomach bloom. Eli isn't mine to be jealous of.

"Um…" I point to the restrooms. "I'll just go there and you can finish your conversation without me."

Eli throws an arm around my shoulders and draws me near. "You're not going anywhere. If anyone should leave, it's Lucinda."

Lucinda huffs. "But…"

"No buts. Enjoy your evening. I know we will." Eli maneuvers me away from her. Once we're out of her hearing range, he stops. "I'm sorry, Lace. I promise I wasn't in a relationship with her. I don't understand why she feels wronged."

I know why. Because Eli is a difficult man to get over. Maybe even impossible.

He kisses my nose. "I promise I have no interest in any other woman than you."

I want to argue with him – we're not in a relationship after all – but the facts are undeniable. He's ignored every other woman tonight. He's made his claim on me clear. I could fall in love with this man.

I freeze. I'm not supposed to fall in love with Eli. I'm supposed to prove to him why we wouldn't make a good couple.

This is not good. This is dangerous for my heart.

What if he forgets about me again? What if this isn't serious to him? Just like our date in high school he completely forgot about?

Chapter 19

"There's only so much willpower in the world and I have none left." ~ Eli

ELI

"What? No limo?" Paisley jokes when we step out of the jet at Jettson's Way.

"What's the point? You aren't impressed by limos."

"It's a vulgar display of wealth."

"You said the same thing about the jet but it didn't stop you from trying every seat, playing with the television, rummaging through the galley, and jumping on the bed."

"I did not jump on the bed."

I wag my phone at her. "I have a video."

Her eyes narrow on me. "Which you will delete if you know what's good for you."

"And miss watching your boobs bounce as you jump? Pass."

She rolls her eyes. "Men and boobs. I'll never understand the attraction."

"Really?" I step closer. "You aren't intrigued by videos of men with six-pack abs?"

"Have you been snooping around my computer?"

I chuckle. "Busted."

We reach my SUV and I open the door for her. Once she's inside, I lean across her to buckle her seatbelt and switch on the seat heating.

"I am perfectly capable of buckling my own seat belt."

I kiss her shoulder. "Let me spoil you. You don't let me buy you things."

He shuts the door before I have a chance to correct him. I don't let it go, though. The second he hops into the driver's seat, I start in on him. "You buy me all kinds of things. A lace shawl that probably cost more than my house. A lunch with a Supreme Court Justice."

"You can't be mad at me for arranging for you to have lunch with a female Supreme Court Justice who's famous for her work on civil rights."

She glares at me. "I can and I am. You spent twenty thousand dollars to win the lunch."

I shrug. "The money is for charity."

"Some people don't earn twenty thousand dollars in an entire year."

"I know. It's depressing." I switch on the car and begin driving home. "Feel free to sleep. I know it's late."

Paisley giggles. "Sleep? I'm too wired to sleep. The keynote speaker was fabulous. I can't stop thinking about what she said about how to make a man into a supporter of equal rights. And the dance performance was marvelous. The music is playing non-stop in the back of my mind. Whoever thought you could perform modern dance to classical music? Not to mention the fabulous food. Those cookies decorated with suffragette sashes were adorable."

I smile. I'm glad she enjoyed herself. I was worried. Especially when the event started with Lucinda claiming we'd been a couple.

I reach across the console to thread my fingers through hers. "Does this mean you'll accompany me more often to these events?"

She shrugs. "Maybe."

I don't push her. The maybe was enough of a hard win. But I'll get her to agree to give me a chance eventually. I'm patient. And I'm not going anywhere. Smuggler's Hideaway is my home now.

She swivels in her seat to face me. "What did you think of the keynote speaker?"

The hour drive back to Smuggler's Hideaway flies by as Paisley dissects the event detail by detail. She already has ideas on how to improve future fundraisers. I'm not surprised. My Lace's mind is always working.

I pull into my driveway and park.

She scans the area. "Where are we? This isn't my house."

"Nope. It's mine."

Her shoulders stiffen. "What are we doing here?"

"I'm not ready for the night to end."

The tension in her body releases. "Me either."

I squeeze her hand before releasing her. "Good."

I jump out of the SUV before scurrying around the front to her side. She already has the door open when I get there.

"I wanted to open the door for you."

She stills. "Shall I shut it again?"

I smile at how adorably confused she appears and grasp her hand to help her out. "Next time, wait for me."

"Who says there's going to be a next time?"

I do, but I'm smart enough to keep my mouth shut.

I lead her to the house and into the living room. "Do you want a nightcap? I have every variety of *Buccaneer's Whiskey* you can imagine."

She considers my question for a moment before shaking her head. "If you drink, you can't drive me home."

I step closer to her. "You could stay here."

The pulse in her neck thumps. "I thought sex was off the table."

I groan. "I would love nothing more than to flip up this dress, bend you over the couch, and have my wicked way with you."

"Sounds like a plan."

"I promised I wouldn't seduce you. I want to show you there's more between us besides sexual chemistry."

"I think you proved your point when you snarled at any man who came within five feet of me."

"I also snarled at the women."

"I appreciate you being an equal opportunity snarler."

I debate pushing the matter, but I want more than a moment with Paisley. I can't have forever. But I want to enjoy her for as long as possible. Having sex tonight is not the best method to get what I want.

I palm her neck. "How about one nightcap and I take you home?"

"What kind of whiskey do you have?"

"Do you drink whiskey?"

"On occasion."

She's perfect. A woman who can match me wit for wit and also drinks whiskey. I couldn't want more. Except to strip her bare and taste every inch of her skin. My cock twitches in agreement. It says forget the whiskey. Good thing it's not in charge.

"I'll pour us some drinks."

It takes every ounce of willpower in my body to step away from her. To walk to the bar and find two glasses. To pour us each a whiskey.

When I return to Paisley and hand her a glass of whiskey, she's studying me with a confused look on her face.

"What's wrong?"

"I'm not certain how to proceed."

I lift my glass. "Usually we clink glasses, make a toast about smugglers and mermaids, and drink our whiskey."

"I mean how to seduce you."

My cock twitches with such vehemence I nearly fall over. "What did you say?"

"I'm not used to seducing men. Or, rather, seducing men is usually as easy as indicating I'm available for a night of pleasure and then they take over."

I growl. "How many men have you had one-night stands with?"

She ignores me. "I guess direct is the way to go." She downs the whiskey in one go and sets the glass on a table. "I'm not wearing any underwear."

I freeze. "What?" I manage to croak out.

"I'm not wearing any underwear. No panties. No bra. Nothing. I am completely naked underneath this dress."

My cock hardens and lengthens. It wants what Paisley is offering. I have one thing to settle first.

I fist her hair. "Are you telling me you spent an entire evening at an event with men staring at you while you were naked underneath your dress?"

"I didn't stutter, although I don't believe men were staring at me. They were too afraid of you."

"As they should be." I tug on her hair. "Were you planning to go to the event in Smuggler's Hideaway without panties on?"

If so, I'll have to punish her. I'll spank her ass until she promises to never ever leave the house without panties on again. No one should have easy access to what is mine.

And make no mistake about it. Paisley is mine. She might not be mine forever. But she's mine for now.

"I was still getting dressed when you arrived."

"You were wearing shoes."

"And? Is there an order for how I should dress? Do shoes always have to be last?"

"Stop joking with me."

"I'm not trying to joke. I'm trying to convince you to have sex with me." She licks her lips. "The idea of you bending me over the sofa is especially appealing."

I groan. "You're making it awful hard to keep my promise not to have sex with you."

She grabs hold of my cock and squeezes. "Yes, it is hard."

"I want to prove to you there's more to us than our chemistry."

"I love chemistry. I have a college degree in chemistry. I think I have enough knowledge of chemistry. Let's move on to the portion of the evening where you provide me with orgasms."

"Orgasms? You want more than one?"

She shrugs. "I want two. I thought you might need a challenge."

"I do love a good challenge."

She nips my bottom lip. "I challenge you, Eli Raider, to give me more than one orgasm tonight."

My blood heats as my hard length presses against my pants – intent on getting to the object of its desires.

"I'll give you as many orgasms as you want tonight."

"Just to be clear, I want at least three."

"You said two before."

"It isn't a challenge unless it's hard."

I press her against the wall and shove my cock against her stomach. "I think I proved it's hard."

Her eyes flare. "You did."

"You want me to bend you over the sofa?"

"Yes, please."

"You won't claim our relationship is based solely on sex?"

"I won't."

I study her. Is she lying? Will she run away tomorrow? With heat pumping through my veins and my cock pulsing to its own beat, I find it difficult to care.

"Fuck it," I murmur before I shackle her wrist and drag her to the sofa. I maneuver her so she's facing it while I'm at her back. I massage those ass checks I'm slowly becoming obsessed with before leaning close to whisper in her ear, "Bend over."

She doesn't hesitate to follow my orders. I gather the silky material of her dress and lift it higher and higher until her bare ass is unveiled. I groan. I'm glad I didn't know she wasn't wearing panties all night. I wouldn't have been able to resist dragging her to the nearest corner and sinking into her.

I place a hand on her lower back. "Bend over for me."

"Widen your legs," I demand once she's bent over the sofa. She spreads her legs and I wish I could take a picture of her this way.

She glances over her shoulder at me and lifts her eyebrow. "I can't orgasm from you staring at me."

I dig my wallet out of my pocket and pull out a condom. I unzip my pants and let them fall to the floor with my underwear. Once I've donned the condom, I notch my cock at her entrance.

"This isn't going to be slow. It's going to be fast and hard."

"Promises. Pro—"

Her taunt is cut off with a moan as I sink into her.

This is where I belong. This is where I'll always belong. Paisley is mine. I'm falling for this stubborn woman who challenges me at every turn.

My throat closes as fear slithers through me. I can't fall in love with Paisley. I can't fall in love with any woman. Not when I can't trust a woman to stay.

Paisley's walls convulse around my cock and I push thoughts of love out of my mind to concentrate on the task at hand. Making Paisley come as many times as possible.

The fear can wait.

Chapter 20

"I can ignore a dare. I can. I just prefer not to." ~ Paisley

PAISLEY

I wake to the feel of Eli gliding the tip of his finger up my back. My naked back. I bite back a groan. I shouldn't have given in to the temptation of Eli. Again.

But after an evening of being jetted off to a fundraiser, watching him growl at anyone who came too near, and enjoying being in his company, I couldn't resist him anymore.

He squeezes my hip and kisses my shoulder. "What are you thinking about so hard this morning?"

"How to extricate myself from this situation without you making a fuss."

He bursts into laughter. He wraps his arms around me and pulls me near as his body trembles with his mirth. It feels entirely too good to be all wrapped up in him.

"I really should leave."

He rolls me until he's looming over me. "Stay for breakfast."

"I'm not much of a breakfast person."

"I have coffee." When I don't give in to the temptation of coffee, he pushes. "I'll give you a tour of my house."

"House or mansion?"

"Home." He kisses my nose before jumping out of bed. "Come on. You'll have the exclusive scoop since I never invite people, who aren't my family, to my house."

"Never?"

He shackles my wrist and tugs me out of bed. "Never."

Damn him. He knows how much I enjoy being the first at anything. And I can't deny I'm curious to see his house. I know he had it built to specification before he moved back to Smuggler's Hideaway.

"I guess I can suffer through a tour of your house if it makes you happy."

He chuckles and holds up a robe. "You can wear this. Unless you want me to ravage you in every room of the house."

I pretend to consider the question. "How many rooms are there?"

"There are seven bedrooms and…"

I hold up a hand. "Enough. I'll wear the robe."

He helps me into the robe and tightens the sash around my waste. "I like you in my robe."

I lift up my arms and wave my hands but they're hidden by the material. "It's a bit big for me."

Eli rolls the material up my right arm until my hand appears before switching to the other arm. "I like you in my robe," he repeats.

I nod to his hardening cock. "I can tell."

He digs a pair of sweatpants out of a drawer and dons them. "You ready for the tour?"

"As long as coffee appears sometime in the near future, I'm ready."

He grasps my hand. "We'll start in the kitchen."

He leads me out of the bedroom and down the stairs to the kitchen. My jaw drops open at the sight of it. "This kitchen is bigger than the one we have at the *Five Fathoms* restaurant."

He shrugs as he makes his way to the coffee machine. "I wanted a kitchen where Mom could prepare holiday meals. With six boys in the family, she needs the extra space." He smirks. "We have a tendency to steal food while she's cooking."

He switches on the coffee machine.

"Are you certain you know how to operate this machine?"

He glares at me. "It's not my fault the coffee machine at the distillery is possessed by the devil."

"Is this a frequent occurrence? Appliances in your life being possessed by the devil? Because rumor has it you ruined the coffee machine at *Apparoo,* too."

He growls. "Who told you?"

I giggle. "Dakota. Your assistant is quite helpful."

"I guess I don't need to wonder how you managed to get in my office to prank me any longer."

I smirk. "You still need to wonder. Dakota didn't help."

"You always were a troublemaker," he mutters as he starts the coffee.

"False. Chloe and Sophia are the troublemakers."

He snorts. "And they forced you to join their shenanigans."

I nod. "Exactly."

"As if anyone could force you to do anything you don't want to," he mutters.

I wish he was correct. But he's not. My evil stepsisters and stepfather have forced me to do many things I didn't want to do. All in the name of family. They don't understand the meaning of family. But I go along with it for the sake of my mother. My stepfather would bully her even worse if I didn't attend certain events.

Eli hands me a cup of coffee. I sniff the brew before taking a small sip. "It's good."

"You don't have to sound surprised."

"Trust me. I've seen what you can do to a coffee machine. I'm not faking surprise."

"Ready for the tour now?"

My nose wrinkles. "I don't know."

The kitchen is impressive. The rest of the house is bound to be amazing. It's a bit intimidating if I'm being honest.

"There's no reason to be scared. Nothing in this house will bite you." He waggles his eyebrows. "Unless you want it to."

I narrow my eyes on him. "No biting."

He winks. "You didn't mind last night."

I feel my cheeks warm but ignore them. "Let's have this tour then. I don't have all day."

He threads his fingers through mine and leads me out of the kitchen. "This is the living room. You might be familiar with the couch."

I am no wilting flower. I draw a finger along the back of the sofa. "It is a nice sofa." I glance up at Eli and bite my bottom lip. "Very comfortable."

He groans. "You can't tease me if I'm not allowed to ravish you in every room of the house."

I quirk up an eyebrow. "Who said I don't want you to ravage me in every room of the house?"

"You can't distract me."

"Distract you?" I flutter my eyelashes. "Whatever do you mean?"

"You want me to give into temptation and bend you over the sofa, so you don't have to discuss how good we are together."

"I agree we're good together."

He steps close and presses his front to mine. "We're fucking spectacular together but there's more to us than chemistry."

My heart thuds in my chest. I'm not ready to admit there's more to us than chemistry. Eli would be too easy to fall in love with. But I've made the mistake of thinking I could fall in love before. And I don't repeat my mistakes.

"Do you really have a swimming pool in the basement?"

He sighs and steps back. "There's only one way to find out." He motions me forward and I scurry in front of him.

We descend to the basement. This time, I don't let my jaw drop to the floor. I clear my throat and feign nonchalance.

"Is this all?" I ask as I scan the area.

Behind a glass wall is a gym facility to rival any professional fitness center I've been to. Next to it is a gurgling hot tub behind which is a sauna. But the real eyecatcher is the pool. It runs the entire length of the house.

"Nova would love this. She's a great swimmer but she's afraid to swim in the ocean."

"You should invite her over. In fact, invite all of your friends over. I'll invite my brothers. We'll have a pool party."

I point to the volleyball net stored in the corner. "I hope you have an industrial sized first aid kit."

"I have five brothers. I have every first aid kit known to man. Plus, my mom's a nurse."

"Handy. It would have been useful for Sophia's mom to be a nurse when we were growing up."

"Sophia's mom?" he asks as he sits in a lounger chair. He tugs on my hand until I sit on his lap.

"What are you doing?"

"Asking you about Sophia's mom."

"We always hung out at Lily's house. Sophia was the only one of us who had a normal family life. Although, she's been in love with her brother's best friend forever. So maybe not completely normal."

He brushes the hair from my face. "I'm sorry your home life wasn't what it should have been."

"Should have been?" I shrug. "It's a waste of time to worry about what should have been. I prefer to concentrate on the future."

"Good." He nods. "Me too." He toys with a strand of my hair. "And the future I want to concentrate on now is a future with you."

I moan. "I should have known you wouldn't let it go."

"What can I say? I'm a man who knows what he wants. And before you ask, what I want is you."

I frown. "You don't want me. You want sex."

"Beep!" He makes a buzzer sound. "Wrong."

"You didn't even remember ghosting me on a date until I reminded you."

He fists my hair and tugs. "I've apologized for my behavior. You've accepted my apology. You can't constantly bring up the past if you want to go forward in the future."

I consider debating with him but I can't. He's not wrong after all. "You are correct."

He chuckles. "And you couldn't resent it more."

I shrug my shoulders. "You're pushing me into a relationship I don't want. I'm allowed to be resentful."

"Don't want? If you can honestly tell me you don't want a relationship with me, I'll retreat. I'll pack you up in my SUV, drive you home, and never bother you again."

My pulse increases as fear spikes within me. No more Eli? No more coffee mornings? No more teasing each other?

He kisses my forehead. "But I don't believe you want me to leave you alone. I think you're scared."

I narrow my eyes on him. "I'm not scared."

Challenge sparkles in his eyes. "Prove it."

"Stop daring me," I snarl.

"Stop fighting me when we want the same thing and I'll stop daring you."

"Liar."

He kisses my jaw. "Give us a chance, Lace." He nibbles along my jaw until he reaches my ear. "I'll make it worth your while."

I wrestle with my answer. I want to say yes. I always want to say yes where Eli's concerned. Even when I hated him, I was drawn to him.

"There's no reason to be afraid."

"I'm not afraid."

"Then, say yes."

"Yes."

I immediately open my mouth to take the word back, but Eli places a finger over my lips. "You won't regret it." He unties my robe and shoves the material off of my shoulders until I'm bared to him. "Let me show you why."

He dips his head to lick my breast and I force my fear into a tiny box in my mind. I'll deal with it later.

Chapter 21

"It's possible I've been outmaneuvered but I'll never admit it out loud." ~ Eli

ELI

"What are we doing here?" Paisley asks as I park at *Mermaid Mystical Gardens.* "I thought we were meeting your family."

"We are. It's family day."

"We're at an amusement park for children."

I quirk up an eyebrow. "And you've never been here with your friends as an adult?"

"You haven't lived on Smuggler's Hideaway for a decade. How do you know everything?"

"The smuggler's grapevine is very thorough."

"Whatever," she mutters before asking, "Why are we here on family day when your youngest brother is old enough to drink?"

"When one of us has a birthday, the person having his birthday gets to choose where to spend the day."

"Whose birthday is it? Why didn't you tell me? I don't have a present."

Panic lights her eyes and I squeeze her hand. "It's Miles' birthday next week. And don't worry. I put your name on my present."

"Miles? I'm surprised he doesn't want to spend the day surfing."

"Trust me, he does. But Mom put her foot down last year when Rhett smacked Zane with a surfboard and gave him a concussion."

I gasp. "A concussion?"

"In Rhett's defense, Zane deserved it. Zane kept teasing him about Dakota."

"What is the deal with Rhett and Dakota anyway? Are they exes?"

"Nope. They're an explosion ready to happen."

She grins. "I do love a good explosion."

"My chemistry nerd."

She scowls at me. "Chemistry is essential to human life. Without chemistry, medicines wouldn't be possible and—"

Instead of explaining how I was teasing her, I stop her rant in another way. I lean across the console and mold my lips to hers. She sighs and I plunge my tongue inside her mouth. Her taste hits me and I growl as I palm her neck to bring her closer.

There's a knock on my window. "Are you joining us or are you going to make out in your car all day?"

I wrest my mouth from Paisley's to glare at Kai.

The door behind me opens and Zane settles in the back seat. "What are you doing?"

He shrugs. "I thought we were meeting in here since you two won't come out."

Miles climbs into the seat behind Paisley. "What are we talking about?"

"Are all of my brothers going to join us in my SUV?"

"It's not our fault you decided to buy a vehicle bigger than the Smuggler's Hideaway school bus," Miles says.

"My SUV is not as big as a bus," I grumble.

Paisley's nose wrinkles. "It is pretty big, though."

Zane and Miles stick their heads between our seats. "What do you know about size, Paisley?" Miles asks.

"Yeah." Zane nods. "Do you know what six inches is?"

She appears adorably confused. "Of course, I do."

Miles rolls his eyes. "Paisley the Perpetual Know It All knows everything."

Paisley shrinks into herself and I growl before slapping Miles on the shoulder. "You do not tease Paisley with a childish nickname."

Miles focuses on Paisley and grimaces. "I'm sorry, Paisley. I didn't think. I won't use the term again. Cross my heart and hope my surfboard doesn't die."

"It's okay," Paisley mumbles.

"No, it's not. You're Eli's now. I should have more respect."

"I don't belong to Eli. Women are not property."

He holds up his hands. "You're Eli's special lady friend now was what I meant to say."

"Special lady friend?" Zane asks. "What are you? Four?"

Miles shoves him. "If I'm four, what are you? A baby?"

"Out of my SUV," I order everyone.

Zane launches himself at Miles, who opens the door and shoves him outside. He tumbles to the ground while laughing.

Paisley observes them. "Are we certain an amusement park is a good idea for them?"

I grin at her. "It'll be fun."

"I don't think your definition and my definition of fun are the same."

"I guess we'll find out." I hop out of the SUV and rush around to open the door for her.

I'm helping her down when Jaxon and Rhett arrive.

"Where's Mom and Stuart?" Rhett asks as he surveys the group.

"If they skipped out on this juvenile event, I will not be amused," Jaxon mutters.

Miles scowls at him. "Could you at least try not to be boring on my birthday?"

"It's not your birthday yet."

I clap my hands. "You know the rules. You have to behave on family day."

"What kind of stupid rule is 'you have to behave'?" Zane asks.

"I agree with Zane," Paisley says. "Behave is incredibly subjective. I'm certain the word behave means drastically different things to Zane than to Rhett."

Rhett grunts in response.

I raise an eyebrow at Paisley. "Do you want to end up stuck in the *Atlantis Adventure* because one of these yahoos jumped out of the boat?"

The *Atlantis Adventure* is a water ride through the lost city of Atlantis. It's for children but my brothers don't care.

She shrugs. "There's a secret exit after the capital city near the hoard of gold."

"Best. Birthday. Ever!" Miles shouts. "We're exploring the lost city of Atlantis."

"Can we play 'I spy'?" Zane asks.

"I'll play," Paisley says. "What's my prize when I win?"

Rhett throws an arm around my shoulders. "She's fitting right in. You worried for nothing."

I never worried about Paisley fitting in with my family. Between the six of us, there's enough diversity for her to feel at home amongst us. No, my concerns with her are different.

"She was too quick to agree to play," Kai says and brings my attention back to their conversation. "She's certain of her win. How about another game?"

Miles waggles his eyebrows. "A drinking game."

Paisley frowns. "I didn't know we were coming here or I would have brought my flask. The prices in the amusement park are obnoxious."

Kai points to me. "Don't worry. Eli pays for everything."

"You shouldn't take advantage of him because he has money."

He shrugs. "What else are we going to do with him? He's pretty useless."

Paisley taps her chin. "I get your point, but he is pretty to look at."

"Gross. He's my brother."

Paisley winks at me. "But he's not my brother."

"Are the two of you going to give each other googly eyes all day?" Zane feigns retching.

She shrugs. "Only if it will bother you."

I throw my arm around Paisley's shoulders. "Come on. Mom and Stuart are here."

We walk as a group toward the entrance to *Mermaid Mystical Gardens.* I slow down to let my brothers get ahead.

I bite Paisley's earlobe. "I'm useless, am I?"

"I didn't say you were useless. I merely said I understood Kai's point of view. I can understand a point of view without agreeing with it."

I sigh. "I'm never going to win an argument with you, am I?"

She smiles. "It's good you learn your limitations now."

We stop at the entrance to the park where my family has gathered. "Paisley, I'd like you to meet my mom. Mom, this is Paisley. Paisley, this is my mother, Jessica."

Paisley extends her hand but Mom pulls her into a hug. "Welcome to the family."

Paisley freezes and I groan. "Way to scare her, Mom."

"What?" she asks as she releases Paisley. "I'm being welcoming to your girlfriend."

"She's not his girlfriend. She's his special lady friend," Miles says.

Mom ignores Miles. "It's lovely to meet you, Paisley. I thought my boys were never going to settle down."

Paisley stiffens and I rub a hand down her back. I wanted Paisley to meet my family because her family are a bunch of assholes. I didn't think Mom would jump straight to weddings and babies. She should know better. I don't plan on ever getting married.

Stuart offers Paisley his hand. "I'm Stuart, Jessica's husband. Welcome to the mad house."

"I thought we agreed on the term asylum," Kai mutters.

Miles rubs his hands together. "Did everyone wear their swimming trunks? I think I've decided our first ride is *Grotto Rapids.*"

"I didn't bring a swimming suit," Paisley says.

"Too bad since the rule states you have to go on every ride I go on."

"And what happens if I don't?"

"You don't get to pick a location for your all day birthday celebration." He points to me. "You can join Mr. Fuddy Duddy. He never celebrates his birthday."

"What if I want to celebrate my birthday by parachuting out of an airplane?" Paisley asks.

"Awesome," Kai says. "I think I love you already."

I growl at him and he raises his hands in the air. "What? Do you not want me to like your special lady friend?"

"I want you to stop referring to her as my special lady friend," I grit out.

Paisley elbows me. "Why? Am I not special? Am I not a lady? Am I not your friend?"

"You're as bad as the rest of them."

"My best friends are Sophia, Chloe, Nova, and Maya. What did you expect?" Her eyes light up. "We should totally ask them to join us."

"Next time. Today is Miles' day."

"Sorry Miles. I didn't mean to distract from your day in the spotlight."

"You didn't. In fact," his eyes sparkle in challenge, "since you're not afraid of heights, why don't we start today's adventure with *Kraken's Drop.*"

Kraken's Drop is a drop tower ride in the shape of a giant sea monster.

"I bet I can ride it more times than you before you vomit," Paisley challenges.

"You're on." They shake hands before hurrying off toward the entrance.

I start to follow but Mom threads her arm through my elbow to slow me down.

"I like her for you, Eli."

"I like her, too."

"Good." She smiles. "I'm glad you're finally over your fear that no woman will stick around. I was worried you were going to die alone."

"Eli!" Miles shouts from up ahead. "We need the tickets."

I grab at the excuse to get away from Mom and her insightfulness.

I hate to disappoint her, but she's wrong. No one sticks around forever. But I'll enjoy Paisley's company while she's here.

I just need to keep my heart encased in steel to stop myself from falling in love and getting my heart broken. Because it would be all too easy to fall in love with Paisley. Especially now that we're beyond the hate.

Chapter 22

"Now I understand why Cinderella wanted a man to save her from her evil stepsisters." ~ Paisley

PAISLEY

"Coming," I shout as I rush to the door. I fling it open. "You're..." The smile drops from my face when I realize my visitor isn't Eli.

"I'm what?" Darcy sasses.

I debate telling her the truth. She's not the person I expected or want to see. But she's not alone. Mom is at the back of her entourage and it pains my mother how we don't get along.

"Where are Luna and Emma?" I ask.

My adorable nieces are the only reason I'm not estranged from Darcy. I have no interest in interacting with my stepsister or her husband. But their two girls? I can't cut them out of my life.

Darcy huffs. "They're observing Sammy. The seal is sitting in your neighbor's yard being a pest."

I smile. My nieces are as nerdy as I was at their age. Darcy has tried to get them interested in beauty pageants but they refuse to get involved. I love those girls.

"Are you going to ask us in?" Regan's question is more a demand than question.

"I wasn't expecting you. I'm going out in a little while."

Darcy pushes her way past me. "We don't need much of your time."

Regan follows Darcy while Mom brings up the rear.

"Hello, dear," she says and kisses my cheek.

"What's going on? Why are you here?" I ask her but she shrugs.

Darcy and Regan settle on the sofa in my living room as if they belong there.

"Aren't you going to offer us a drink?" Regan asks.

"I'll have a martini," Darcy orders.

If she thinks I'm going to act as her personal bartender, she will be disappointed.

"If you want a martini, there are plenty of bars in Smuggler's Rest," I say.

She sighs. "A wine will do."

I cross my arms over my chest and glare down at her and Regan. "What are you doing here?"

"Geez. There's no reason to be hostile. You're our sister. Why wouldn't we be here?" Darcy can feign confusion all she wants. I know the truth. Her and Regan never treated me as a sister.

"Let me rephrase. What do you want?"

"I want a martini," Darcy mutters. "But apparently you don't know how to make one."

"A classic martini is a simple recipe consisting of gin and vermouth. Vodka is also an option. It's made by—"

Darcy throws her hand up. "Stop! I was only joking."

Regan snorts. "You should know better. Paisley is the perpetual know it all after all."

"Girls," Mom berates. "Be nice."

"I'm not the one who refuses to provide drinks to her guests," Darcy says.

"You're not a guest. A guest is invited. You showed up uninvited."

Regan groans. "Talking to a robot would be easier."

"You. Are. Not. A. Guest," Darcy mimics a robot, and they dissolve into giggles.

This is my childhood all over again. Since the moment Mom married Conrad, Darcy and Regan teased and tortured me. They never bothered to try and get along with me. I was five years old and they didn't try to be nice.

I sigh and push my glasses up my nose.

"Uh oh. She's fiddling with her nerdy glasses," Regan says between giggles.

I drop my hand with a growl. I open my mouth to argue with them about my glasses but what's the use? If it's not my glasses, it'll be my looks or my clothes or my job or my house or literally anything. They can always find a reason to make fun of me.

I check the time. "I have an appointment."

"She has an appointment," Regan says in a stilted voice.

I bite my tongue before I tell them my voice doesn't resemble a robot. But I don't want to be pulled into their antics. I want nothing to do with them.

If they won't leave, I will.

"I'm going to say hi to Luna and Emma." I start for the door.

"But we haven't had a chance to catch up yet," Regan says.

"Catch up?"

Why would I want to catch up with them? We see each other on birthdays and holidays. In between those times, we have no contact with each other. I'm not even allowed to babysit my nieces. And if I happen upon my stepfather anywhere on the island, he pretends I don't exist.

"You do know what catch up is, don't you?" Darcy asks.

"She's smart but her social skills..." Regan shakes her head.

I tap my foot. "Can you get to the point of your visit?"

"We're wondering how you're doing," Darcy says.

"Yes. It must have been hard when your brewery was destroyed during the hurricane."

I narrow my eyes on Regan. "The hurricane happened over a month ago."

And they didn't lift a hand to help or offer any sympathy at the time. While nearly all of the inhabitants of Smuggler's Rest showed up to help us remove the debris, my family was absent. As usual.

"I'm sorry, dear," Mom says. "I wanted to come but..." She trails off with a wave of her hand.

"But Conrad forbade it."

I hate how my stepfather controls her. He berates her and denigrates her but she remains devoted to him. I have no idea why. I would never let a man treat me the way he treats her.

"Yes, well," Mom glances away. She knows how I feel about Conrad.

"Not all of us want to be alone forever," Regan sneers.

My brow wrinkles. "Aren't you divorced?"

"Not the point."

"What is the point?"

"You shouldn't make fun of Mom for not wanting to be alone," Darcy answers.

I grit my teeth. I hate when Darcy or Regan refer to my mom as their mom. They only call her mom to anger me. Usually, they call her by her name, Eleanor.

"Exactly." Regan nods. "Not all of us want to smash the patriarchy and die all alone with five cats who eat our face off."

"Cats don't actually eat humans."

Darcy rolls her eyes. "Of course, you would focus on the stupid cats."

"I don't have a cat."

Regan pounds a fist on the sofa. "It's not about the cats."

I massage my temple where I feel a headache coming on. "Can you get to the point of this conversation? I have somewhere I need to be."

Darcy snorts. "You have somewhere you need to be? You finished work. Where could you possibly be going?"

"Yeah," Regan continues. "It's not as if you have friends."

I don't bother to explain I have friends. For some reason, they're convinced I lead a sad, pathetic life.

"And you do? Didn't your husband run off with your best friend?"

Regan flicks her hair over her shoulder. "Remi wasn't my best friend."

Darcy pats her hand. "You're better off without him."

Regan sniffs and lifts her nose in the air. "He didn't deserve me."

"You'll find someone new."

"I will."

The answer sounds calculating. What is she up to? Why are my stepsisters here?

"Aunt Paisley! Aunt Paisley!" Luna and Emma shout in unison as they barge into the house. They rush to me and I hug them.

"We saw…"

"Sammy. He was…"

"…next door!"

I smile. It's intriguing how the twins finish each other's sentences.

"What was he doing?"

Luna's nose wrinkles and Emma frowns. "Nothing." They answer in unison.

"We added his location …"

"…to the Sammy spotting app."

The seal is a bit of a celebrity on Smuggler's Hideaway. Tourists come to the island specifically to observe him. It may seem odd, but Sammy is a character. He enjoys lounging in the middle of the road and preens when he's given attention. He also pushes garbage cans over and stalks the customers at the fishmonger.

"Did you—"

"Girls," Darcy interrupts. "Go wash your hands."

"We didn't…"

"…touch the seal."

"You shouldn't…"

"…touch wildlife."

Darcy purses her lips. She finds their antics 'trying'. She's disappointed her daughters don't want to be beauty queens. I'm a scientist. I don't believe in karma. But if I did, I'd say karma found a way to get her back for how she treated me when we were younger.

"Nonetheless." Darcy shoos the twins toward the hallway. "Clean up."

They hurry down the hallway, giggling the entire way.

There's a knock on the door. It should be Eli. He's picking me up before we attend drunk poker with my friends.

"Finally," Emma mutters.

I narrow my eyes on her. "What are you up to?"

She bats her eyelashes. "Nothing."

I don't believe her but there's another knock on the door before I can quiz her further.

"Eli," I greet when I open the door.

He presses his lips to mine. "Are you ready?"

"I have company." I motion him inside and lead him to the living room.

"Is this Eli?" Regan asks with a breathy voice.

Now I understand why my evil stepsisters showed up today. Regan thinks she can steal Eli away from me the same way Darcy stole Ryan from me.

My heart spasms. Will Eli fall into her trap?

Chapter 23

"I'm really hoping this is some kind of fever dream." ~ Eli

ELI

At the predatory look in the woman's eyes, I frown. Who are these people?

"How do you know who Eli is?" Paisley asks.

"We saw a picture of the two of you in the society column at a fundraiser," the woman says.

"It was nice of him to allow you to accompany him," another woman says.

"Allow her?" I ask.

The first woman rolls her eyes. "It's not as if the two of you are a couple."

Paisley flinches, and I wrap an arm around her shoulders. "As a matter of fact, we are a couple."

"For now," the first woman mutters under her breath.

An older woman stands and approaches us. Her eyes are the exact same shade of hazel as Paisley's. This must be her mother.

"I'm Eleanor, Paisley's mom." She offers me her hand.

"It's nice to meet you." It's not nice but Paisley's family being here saves me a trip to visit them.

She waves to the two women. "This is Regan and Darcy."

When Regan reaches toward me, I step back. I have no interest in touching the woman who tortured Paisley during her childhood.

"Are you nearly finished?" I ask Paisley. "We need to get going."

"Where are you going?" Darcy asks.

"Maybe we can come with," Regan adds.

"Sorry," I say. "It's a family event."

"Family event?" Darcy snarls. "We're her family."

"Are you the one who stole Paisley's boyfriend and married him?"

She rolls her eyes. "I didn't steal Ryan. You can't steal a person."

"It's true," two young girls say in unison from behind me.

"Dad says…"

"…he effed up."

"He should have…"

"Girls," Darcy growls. "Do not finish that sentence if you know what's good for you."

They shrug in unison.

Paisley smiles at them. "Eli, these are my nieces, Luna and Emma."

"We're twins!"

"Really?" I feign surprise. "You don't resemble each other in the least."

They giggle. "Your boyfriend is funny."

"Luna, Emma, go wait in the car," Darcy says.

"But Mom."

I chuckle at how adorable they are.

"Do you want children?" I ask Paisley.

Her eyes widen and she rears back. "You're asking me this now? In front of these people?"

Yep. It's the perfect way to telegraph to her stepsisters how serious we are. And, hopefully, prevent Regan from executing whatever scheme she's concocted.

I shrug. "What's the big deal? I can ask you again later if you prefer."

"I prefer."

'She must have hired him," Regan announces.

"Hired me? I own two businesses. I'm not an employee."

She nods. "Exactly. You're a billionaire. You wouldn't date my sister."

"Why not? What's wrong with your sister?"

"We love Aunt Paisley," Luna and Emma say.

"Do you always speak in unison?"

"No. Sometimes we..."

"...finish each other's sentences."

"I'm glad none of my brothers were twins. They were enough trouble as it was."

Luna bats her eyelashes while Emma widens her eyes. "We're not trouble."

Darcy crosses her arms over her chest and glares at her children. "Which is why you went to wait in the car when I asked you to."

"But we want to know how many children Aunt Paisley is having," Luna says.

"We want cousins to play with," Emma adds.

Darcy's nostrils flare. "Go wait in the car."

The twins study their mom for a long second before whirling around and running out of the house. "Bye, Aunt Paisley. Bye, Uncle Eli."

Warmth slams into my chest. *Uncle Eli.* I want to be their uncle Eli. I want to be Paisley's family.

I shove those thoughts away. Family doesn't stay. Family can leave. Family can destroy your heart.

I squeeze Paisley's hand. "We should be going. We don't want to be late."

"You don't have to pretend any longer," Darcy says. "The children are gone now. You can let Paisley go."

"We're not pretending," Paisley says.

Regan rolls her eyes. "Yeah, sure. This isn't Cinderella. The nerdy stepsister doesn't get the billionaire."

"Did you ever read Cinderella?" Paisley asks.

"Are you saying I can't read? Just because I'm not a nerd the way you are, doesn't mean I can't read," Regan spits out.

"There's more to life than books." Darcy rakes her gaze over Paisley. "Such as taking care of yourself."

"A little makeup wouldn't hurt," Regan says.

"And some fashion sense."

Regan opens her mouth to speak again but I hold up a hand. "Aren't you going to stop this?" I ask Paisley's mother.

Eleanor wrings her hands together. "They're only teasing."

"This is not teasing," I grumble. "They're being cruel to your daughter, your own flesh and blood, and you're standing there allowing it to happen. You're supposed to be Paisley's mom."

"She's our mother, too," Regan claims.

"Then, she should have taught you to be nice."

She bats her eyelashes. "I can be nice."

"Not nice to a man to get what you want but nice to your sister."

She flicks her hand. "Paisley knows we're teasing."

"I can't believe you put up with this," I say to Paisley.

"I only see them on holidays or birthdays or when they want something."

I don't have to ask what they want. Darcy stole Paisley's college boyfriend so now Regan thinks she can steal Paisley's current boyfriend. Good thing I'm not an idiot the way Paisley's ex obviously is.

"Is it someone's birthday?" I ask.

"Nope."

"And it's not a holiday. I guess it's time for them to leave then."

Her eyes widen in surprise. "You want them to leave?"

I pinch her chin. "Do you want them to stay?"

Her nose wrinkles and I can't resist kissing it. "No."

"Then, they should leave."

At my announcement, warmth floods Paisley's eyes and happiness radiates from her. I want to make her happy every day. Especially when it's as easy as kicking her evil stepsisters and worthless mother out of her house.

Regan stomps her foot. "This is bullshit."

"Let me guess. Someone isn't used to not getting what she wants."

Paisley giggles. "Except her husband left her for her best friend."

"My husband did not leave me for my best friend," Regan shrieks.

"Oh, I'm sorry." Paisley bites her lip and looks contrite. Little liar is a terrible actress. "Do I have the terminology incorrect? What is the proper terminology when your husband starts living with your best friend?"

"Maybe I kicked him out first."

Paisley's brow wrinkles as if she's confused. "Does the sequence matter? Since he started living with her immediately it doesn't seem as if it does. I could be wrong."

"You bitch!" Regan screams and lunges for Paisley.

I step in front of her and hold up my hand. "Touch Paisley and we're going to have more problems than we already do."

"Come on." Darcy pushes Regan toward the door. "We might as well leave. It's obvious Paisley has him brainwashed. There's no other way a billionaire would date her."

I start to correct her, but there's no use. Paisley's stepsisters are delusional if they think they're better than Paisley. Paisley is everything – brains and beauty plus she's funny and phenomenal in bed. She's the whole package.

Eleanor rushes to follow Darcy and Regan. "It was lovely meeting you," she says as she passes us.

"I wish I could say the same."

"Eli," Paisley growls.

"What? I'm not going to pretend I enjoyed meeting your mother when she literally stood there and allowed her husband's grown daughters to be nasty to you."

"I'm sorry, Mom."

"Do not apologize on my behalf. I'm not sorry."

Paisley elbows me. "Be nice."

"I don't want to be nice to someone who allowed you to be bullied while you were growing up."

She throws her hands in the air. "You're incorrigible."

"You might not like me," Paisley's mom says, "but I like you for my girl. She deserves the best."

"She deserves a mom who fights for her."

Her nose wrinkles. It reminds me of Paisley. "I'm not a fighter." A car honks outside. "I better…" She rushes off.

I shut and lock the door behind her.

"You shouldn't—"

Paisley throws herself at me. "Thank you." She rains kisses on my face. "Thank you. You're the best man a special lady friend could ask for."

I grunt. "Please don't say special lady friend."

"But your eye twitches whenever I do. It's fascinating."

I shake my head. "I've created a monster."

She beams up at me. She can tease me about being my special lady friend as much as she wants if it makes her this happy. This woman has me wrapped around her finger.

I nearly startle. I was supposed to keep my heart safe from this woman. Not hand it to her in a giftwrapped package.

Crap. She's going to break my heart when she leaves me.

Chapter 24

"I call your bluff." ~ Paisley

PAISLEY

I stop Eli halfway up the driveaway to Sophia's mom's house. "I need to preemptively apologize for everything that transpires here tonight."

He grins. "What exactly do you think is going to transpire to require an apology?"

"My friends do not hold back."

"Don't worry." He kisses my nose. "I went to high school with your friends. I know exactly how rowdy they can get."

"I didn't use the word rowdy."

He raises an eyebrow. "Are you denying they can be rowdy? Because I remember the time they walked out of a home economics class with you and started a protest outside the window. You made such a racket the teacher had to stop the class."

"Ms. Zimmerman should have met our demands."

"You demanded the class be removed from the curriculum. She would have been out of a job."

"Home economics is a ridiculous class. And it has nothing to do with economics."

"Admit it. The name bugs you more than learning how to cook or sew."

"The name does not bother me more than being forced to carry around a fake baby for a week to prove I knew how to raise a child. If they were worried about sixteen year olds having children, they should have taught us how to use condoms."

"They tried and you made cartoon animal balloons out of them."

I huff. "It wasn't my fault. Chloe dared me."

"Sure, let's blame it all on Chloe."

"It is her fault," I insist.

"Are you two coming inside?" Sophia shouts from the doorway. "The window isn't big enough for all of us to spy on you from."

Chloe joins her. "And we can't hear what you're saying."

"You've been warned," I murmur to Eli before walking to the house.

We gather in the living room with my friends and their partners.

"You know my friends – Sophia, Nova, Maya, and Chloe."

Eli nods in greeting to them.

"And I believe you know Hudson and Caleb since they attended high school at the same time as we did."

He shakes Caleb's hand. "Thank you for your service."

Caleb grimaces but Maya pinches his hip. "What do you say in response?"

"Thank you for paying your taxes?"

She sighs. "I've done my best with him."

I continue the introductions. "And you know Flynn." I narrow my eyes. "Since the two of you colluded to build the brewery inside the distillery."

"Colluded?" Eli chuckles. "We're not Nazi war criminals."

"No. You're much too young." I motion to Chloe's husband. "And this is Lucas. He's a police officer."

Eli shakes his head. "I couldn't believe it when my brothers told me the wild child married a cop."

Lucas throws an arm around Chloe's shoulders. "My wildcat couldn't resist me. It's why she showed up at my house in a raincoat with nothing underneath."

Chloe leans into him. "You would have ripped the raincoat off of me if Natalia wasn't there."

"Who's Natalia?" Eli asks.

"Our daughter." My stomach warms at Chloe's answer. She used to be afraid to have children but now she claims Lucas's daughter as her own. I've enjoyed watching her grow into the woman I always knew she could be.

"This is everyone." My brow wrinkles. "Oh wait. Where's Weston?"

"Scarlett wasn't feeling well and he didn't want to leave her alone," Sophia answers.

"Your brother has changed."

Lucas snorts. "Tell me about it. Patrol with him used to be all about him hitting on women and now it's all about Scarlett this, Scarlett that."

"It's good you have two police officers in your friend group," Eli says.

I smack him. "Why do we need police officers?"

"You know exactly why."

The kitchen door swings open and Lily hurries into the living room while fixing her hair. Jack follows her with a grin on his face.

Sophia moans. "My parents have been making out in the kitchen again."

"What's wrong? Are you jealous? Do you want to go make out in the kitchen?" Flynn waggles his eyebrows at her.

"Is this him?" Lily asks and makes a beeline for Eli.

"This is Sophia's mom," I introduce. "She gave us a safe place to misbehave while we were growing up."

"Good. You needed one since your mother didn't keep you safe."

"You've met Paisley's mother, Eleanor?" Lily asks.

Eli scowls. "If you can call her a mother."

Lily smiles. "He has my seal of approval. Although, I always assumed you'd be in a polyamorous relationship."

I groan. "Lily."

She bats her eyelashes. "What?"

"I'm Lily's husband." Jack offers his hand to Eli. "She's as much as a troublemaker as these kids."

Lily huffs. "I am not a troublemaker."

"And you didn't bring up how Paisley enjoyed watching orgy porn when she was young either."

"I insinuated. You're the one who brought it up."

My cheeks warm. "Can we stop discussing porn now? And, for the record, it isn't as if I was watching porn constantly as a teenager."

Eli shrugs. "I was."

Chloe barks out a laugh. "He has my stamp of approval."

Unlike Chloe, I don't enjoy being the center of attention – especially when we're discussing my watching porn as a teenager. I need to move this conversation on. "Are we going to play drunk poker or are we going to stand around all night?"

Chloe raises her hand. "I vote for standing around making fun of you all night."

Eli squeezes my hand. "Paisley's had enough teasing after a visit from her stepsisters."

"The evil stepsisters came to your house?" Maya asks. "Why?"

"The oldest one, Wicked Regan, thinks she can steal me away from Paisley," Eli answers.

Sophia shakes her head. "Those two always were delusional. Thinking they're prettier than Paisley when they both need a boatload of make-up to hide all of their moles and hooked noses."

As much as I appreciate my friends rallying around me, I don't want to discuss my family. I want to spend the evening having a good time with my friends. Not dissecting everything my stepsisters said and did.

"I'm going to win poker tonight," I announce.

Nova giggles. "You always win."

"Not tonight." Eli rubs his hands together. "I've been playing poker with my brothers since they were old enough to hold cards."

I narrow my eyes on him. "You're on."

Lily ushers us to the dining room where the poker table is set. She picks up a tray filled with whiskey shots and hands them out.

Maya holds up a hand. "No, thank you. I'm not drinking."

I frown at her. "I told you it's perfectly safe to consume one drink while you are trying to conceive."

"Maybe I'm not trying anymore."

Oh no. Is Caleb's recovery backsliding? I thought he was on track since he's been attending therapy.

"Why did you stop…" I trail off when I notice her smile. "You're pregnant?"

She nods. "I wasn't planning on telling anyone yet."

I cringe. "I'm sorry."

Caleb wraps an arm around her waist and draws her near. "There's no reason to be sorry. Maya's been feeling guilty for not telling everyone she's pregnant. She wanted to wait until she's in her second trimester but she felt bad about not telling everyone."

"This is the best news ever." Nova pushes Caleb out of the way to hug Maya. "Our babies are going to grow up together."

Maya wipes at the tears leaking from her eyes. "It's everything we ever wanted."

Caleb growls. "No more crying."

"I can't help it, soldier. I'm just so happy."

"Bunny," he murmurs as he enfolds her in his arms and sways her from side to side.

"I'm happy, too." Lily waves her hands in front of her face. "Another grandchild."

"Don't cry, sweet flower," Jack murmurs before hauling her near.

She pushes him away. "We need to drink shots."

"Hear! Hear!" Chloe and Sophia shout in unison.

Lily passes out the whiskey shots. "Lift your glasses. To smugglers, bootleggers, rumrunners."

"And the mermaids who loved them!" We finish as one before downing the shots.

"I thought you didn't believe in mermaids," Eli says as he holds out a chair for me.

"It's not a question of believing. Mermaids don't exist."

He shakes his head as he sits next to me. "And you call yourself a smuggler."

"She is a smuggler," Sophia says. "Remember the time she smuggled moonshine into the school assembly."

Nova nods. "I remember. It was eleventh grade."

"It was my first ever hangover," Chloe says.

Maya groans. "I was sick to my stomach."

Lily clicks her tongue. "All of you were sick. I had buckets set up all over the floor of the basement since none of you could aim to save your lives. I didn't think I'd ever get rid of the smell in the basement."

Maya clutches her stomach. "Don't remind me."

Eli chuckles. "I didn't figure Paisley would be the one of this group to sneak alcohol into school."

"It was revenge," I explain. "Darcy was home from college. She had a stash of moonshine she didn't think anyone knew about. I stole it but she couldn't accuse me since she'd have to admit to not being daddy's perfect little princess."

He growls. "I seriously hate your family."

My stomach flips. No man has ever defended me to my family before. I've never had good luck with boyfriends and my family. The last boyfriend I introduced to my family dumped me for my sister.

Regan thought it would be easy to steal Eli from me. After all, all Darcy had to do was crook her finger and Ryan tripped over himself to get to her.

But Eli's different. He's not easily deterred. He doesn't run away from my crazy friends. He doesn't put up with my shitty family. He sticks around and holds my hand the entire time.

Maybe love isn't so scary after all.

Chapter 25

ELI

Paisley stops at her door and glances over her shoulder at me. "Do you want to come in?"

My cock twitches. Hell, yeah, I do.

I whirl her around to face me. "Yes," I murmur before molding my lips to hers. I thrust my tongue into her mouth and she melts into me. She fits perfectly against me. As if she was made for me.

I explore her mouth while enjoying her sweet taste. The bite of exotic is perfect for Paisley. She's sweet but she's exceptional in every way. She's unique. She's my Lace.

"Lace," I whisper against her lips. "We need to go inside."

She startles before pulling away from me. She scans the street. "It's a good thing my nosy neighbor isn't home."

"Isn't Maya one of your neighbors?"

"Exactly."

I chuckle.

She unlocks her door and leads me inside. "Do you want a nightcap?"

I maneuver her until she's pressed up against the wall. "I want you." I press my hard length against her stomach and her eyes flair.

"This is convenient since I want you, too."

I tuck a strand of her hair behind her ear. As usual, her curly hair has escaped her ponytail. I love how uncontrollable her hair is. The same as she is.

"But we need to have a talk first."

She squeezes my ass. "Must we?"

"We must."

"If you're going to whine about losing at poker, can we skip it?"

I tweak her nose. "I don't whine."

She raises her eyebrows. "Do you prefer the word grumble? Grouse? Gripe?"

I slap a hand over her mouth. "I don't need you to list every synonym of whine known to man since I didn't whine."

She peels my hand away. "But you did lose."

"You could have warned me you're a poker shark."

"I did say I was going to win."

True. She did. "I'm not used to losing when playing poker."

She smirks. "Why don't we play a round of strip poker?"

Based on how well she played earlier, I'll be naked in no time. Huh. Not a bad idea. But first.

"We do need to talk."

"What about?"

I lead her to the sofa. Once I'm seated, I pull her on my lap.

"The last time we were in this position, I ended up with red legs."

I grin. "I know. I remember."

I will never forget my first time with Paisley. I went from thinking she hated me to wanting to spend all my time buried in her tight heat. I roll my hips and she gasps when my hardness hits her core.

"If you want to talk, this isn't the way to go about it." She clutches my shoulders and grinds down on my cock. "Scratch what I said. This is the way to go."

I moan as she moves above me. As much as I want to strip her bare and sink into her, we do need to talk. I grasp her hips to stop her movements.

"Fine." She sighs. "What do you want to talk about?"

"Do you need another man?"

Her brow wrinkles. "Another man? I thought I had one. Namely, you. Is this your way of breaking up with me? It's quite confusing. You should work on your break-up speech."

I pinch her hip. "I'm not breaking up with you. I'm trying to discuss your sexual needs."

"And you think I need another man? Our sexual encounters have been extremely satisfying. I don't need a different man."

"No. Not a different man. Another man. In addition to me."

Her eyes widen. "You want to have a threesome?"

I grit my teeth. I do not want to have a threesome but if it's what she needs to be satisfied, I'll figure it out.

"No, I don't. But do you?"

"You're asking if I want a threesome?"

I nod. "Considering your porn viewing preferences."

"My porn viewing preferences?" Her eyes widen. "Oh. You're referring to the orgies I watched when I was younger."

"Yes."

"Why didn't you say as much to begin with? You were being all mysterious. I was already drafting my letter for the 'worst breakup ever' column in the *Smuggler's Gazette*."

I palm her face. "I'm serious, Lace. Do you need a threesome to be sexually satisfied?"

"I love how concerned you are about this but I'm good."

"And the orgy porn?"

She shrugs. "I was fourteen and didn't understand where all the parts went."

I laugh. "Where all the parts went?"

"The porn was research. Which Lily knows very well since I told her as much when she gave me the polyamorous relationship sex talk. But she conveniently forgets whenever she wants to tease me."

"I wish I could have been a fly on the wall when Sophia's mom explained polyamorous relationships to you."

"All men do," she mutters.

"To be clear...you are perfectly fine being in a traditional male/female relationship with no need to add sexual partners?"

"This is correct." She cups my cock and squeezes. "Now, can we move on to the next portion of our evening when you give me multiple orgasms?"

"You are a demanding little thing."

She shrugs. "I know what I want."

"Same, Lace, same," I whisper before drawing her close until her chest hits mine.

She pushes against me. "Don't you want a bed?"

"I have a lot of good memories of you and couches." I wink.

Her eyes heat. "Same but I'm in the mood for a bed."

"If my woman wants a bed, my woman gets a bed."

I lift her from my lap and stand. "Lead the way."

I follow her down the hallway to her bedroom. It's a simple room with a bed, two dressers, and bedside tables piled with books. There is one whimsical aspect, though. The bed is a canopy.

"I didn't expect you to have a canopy bed."

"Darcy and Regan both had them growing up, but I wasn't allowed to get one. When I bought my first bed, I got a canopy." Paisley shrugs but her eyes fill with pain.

I wrap my arms around her and draw her near. "That's the last time you mention their names when we're in bed together. I don't want them spoiling our time together."

"We're not in bed together. We're standing next to the bed."

"Be good or I won't let you come."

She sniffs. "I'll come when I want to. Assuming you stop talking at some point."

"Are you teasing me, Lace?" I trail my hands down her sides until I reach the hem of her t-shirt. "Lift your arms." She does and I draw the t-shirt up her body. I throw it behind me.

She's wearing a lacy white bra. I trace the edge of the lace with a finger. "This is pretty but I prefer it when you're naked underneath your clothes. Fewer barriers to your skin."

I reach around and snap open her bra. I push the straps down her arms and let it fall to the floor. "Better," I murmur as I begin to knead and massage her breasts.

She arches her back to push her chest closer to me. "Do you enjoy it when I play with your pretty titties?"

"Do you need to ask?"

"I love how your breath hitches whenever I talk dirty."

"My…" Her argument is cut off when I pinch her nipple. She gasps and rubs her legs together.

"What's wrong, Lace? Do you need something?"

"You promised me multiple orgasms."

"As I recall, I didn't promise. You demanded."

"Same thing."

I enjoy bantering with Paisley, but I want to make her breathless. I want her mindless with desire and unable to speak in coherent sentences.

I trail my hand down her stomach. I snap open her jeans and sneak my hand under her panties. She widens her legs to give me room to maneuver.

I bite and nibble along her chin until I reach her ear. "What do you want, Lace? My fingers?"

She grasps my wrist and tries to push my hand down. I resist. "You have to tell me what you want."

"I was showing you."

"Tell me," I demand.

She grits her teeth, but she doesn't speak. I nibble on her earlobe. "Tell me, Lace. Say the word and I'll give you the world."

"Fingers," she grumbles. "I want your fingers."

I plunge two fingers into her pussy and she moans long and hard. Now we're getting somewhere. I start to thrust and her fingernails dig into my shoulders as she meets my thrusts.

"I love how wet your pussy is for me."

Her walls tighten around me.

"This first one is going to be quick. I can't wait to sink into you."

I quicken my pace as I use the palm of my hand to press against her clit. She begins to pant.

"Say my name when you come."

"I'm…"

"Say my name," I growl.

Her walls tighten and flutter around my fingers as her climax hits.

"Eli," she moans.

I continue to pump in and out of her until her orgasm wanes. She slumps against me and I kiss her hair. "That's one."

"Mmm…"

Nearly speechless is good, but I want her screaming my name before the night is over.

I remove my fingers before shoving her jeans and panties down her legs. Once she's naked, I pat her ass. "Get on the bed. On your back. Arms above your head holding onto the headboard."

She narrows her eyes at me. "You're bossy."

"And you love it." I kiss her nose. "Now, get your fine ass into the bed. I need to give you a few more orgasms."

She glares at me for a moment longer before climbing into the bed. "I want at least two more orgasms."

I dig out my wallet and remove a condom.

"We don't need those," Paisley says and I freeze. I've never had sex without a condom before.

"We don't?"

"I'm on the pill and I'm clean."

"I'm clean, too."

"Good. Then we can dispense with condoms."

My cock twitches. It's excited by the idea of sinking into Paisley without a barrier.

"Are you sure?"

"We're exclusive, aren't we?"

I growl. "No other man touches you while we're together."

"And no other woman touches you while we're together."

"I don't want another woman touching me."

"Good. It's decided. No condoms necessary."

I rip off my t-shirt and shove my jeans down my legs.

Paisley giggles. "Are you in hurry?"

"This is going to be quick." I climb on top of her and notch my cock at her entrance.

She wraps her legs around my waist. "Not too quick. You promised multiple orgasms."

"I'll get you off with my mouth later," I promise before sinking into her.

I don't stop until I'm fully seated. This is the best feeling in the world. Better than a bank account with nine zeros. Better than having a successful business. Better than being able to afford to buy Mom a house.

Nothing can top this.

Chapter 26

"I don't know how to be lazy." ~ Paisley

PAISLEY

I snuggle into Eli. I'm not ready to wake up and face the day. I could lie here forever in his arms.

Lie forever in Eli's arms? My heart races and my palms sweat. Do I want to be with Eli forever?

Eli kisses my shoulder and I force those scary thoughts away. "Good morning, Lace."

I groan. "I don't want to get up."

"Then, don't. You own your own business. You can play hooky sometimes."

"It's not my own business. I'm not the sole owner."

"I bet Maya, Nova, Chloe, and Sophia wouldn't complain if you skip a day."

True. They wouldn't. "There's too much to do. I can't leave my beer without supervision for the day."

His body moves against mine as he chuckles. "Is your beer going to be naughty if left unsupervised?"

I elbow him. "I'm serious. It's important to keep a close watch on the brewing process."

"You could have your assistant watch over your precious beer."

I consider his question. I've been training Blossom to handle several of my tasks. Except developing new recipes. It's my favorite aspect of my work and I will never hand it over to another person.

"Blossom's not ready yet," I conclude.

"You don't know until you throw her in the deep end."

My nose wrinkles. "I'm not fond of the throw a person in the deep end management philosophy."

Eli rolls me over until we're facing each other. "How about this? Let her handle things this morning. We can have a lazy morning and it will give her an opportunity to prove herself."

"A lazy morning?"

He brushes my hair out of my face. "You do know how to be lazy, don't you?"

"Not really. But it's of no concern. You can't be lazing around all morning. You have two businesses to run."

"I don't run *Apparoo*. I'm merely the Chief Financial Officer."

"Merely the Chief Financial Officer of a company worth several billion dollars? I'm concerned you don't understand the meaning of the word merely."

"Smartass." He tickles my ribs.

I bat him away. "Stop."

His eyes light up. "Are you ticklish?"

"I don't enjoy being tickled." His fingers pause. "At least a third of people do not enjoy being tickled."

"I'm sorry, Lace." He kisses my cheek. "I won't tickle you if you don't enjoy it."

"Thank you."

He cups his ear. "What did you say? I couldn't hear you over the sound of your stomach grumbling."

I smack him. "I'm hungry. I'm always hungry after a night of winning poker."

"Don't gloat or I won't make you breakfast."

I perk up. "You can cook?"

"I practically raised my five younger brothers. Those heathens demanded food three times a day. We didn't have money for going out or getting take-out, so I learned to cook."

At his admission, guilt swamps me. "I'm sorry."

His brow wrinkles. "Sorry for what?"

"I shouldn't make fun of your wealth. I understand the need for financial stability given your background. I will cease to joke about your money."

He smiles. "There's no need to apologize. I don't have money issues. I didn't become a billionaire because I have this deep driven desire to have financial security."

"How did you become a billionaire then?"

"Luck. Pure and simple." I motion for him to explain. "Jeremy was my roommate at college. When he developed his first app, he asked me for a loan to market it. I gave him my tuition money and the rest is history."

"I agree luck was involved, but you're a smart person. You wouldn't have loaned Jeremy the money if you didn't believe in him."

"I'm a smart person." He preens.

I roll my eyes. "Don't gloat. It's unbecoming."

"I happen to know you find me incredibly becoming."

"Only because you're good at giving orgasms."

He barks out a laugh. "I never know what you're going to say." He hops out of bed. "Come on. I'll make you some breakfast."

He saunters toward the hallway. "Are you going to cook naked?"

He shrugs. "It's a lazy morning. Lazy mornings are conducted nude."

"At least put on your briefs."

He waggles his eyebrows. "Afraid you won't be able to resist me if I'm naked?"

I am. But I won't admit it to him. He's already preening more than the peacock at *Barnacles & Barnyards,* the petting zoo on Smuggler's Hideaway.

"More worried you'll get grease on your penis and I'll be forced to listen to you whine about your pain all day long."

"My penis thanks you for your concern."

"It has been instrumental in providing me with orgasms."

He laughs as he slips on his briefs. They're tight and don't leave anything to the imagination. Maybe I should have insisted he wear jeans.

He opens his arms wide. "Am I suitably dressed to cook you breakfast now?"

"It depends on what you cook."

"It depends on what ingredients you have in your cupboards."

"Why don't you rummage around my cupboards while I get ready?"

He sighs. "There's no chance of you agreeing to have a nude lazy morning?"

I shake my head. I'm not a prude. I have no problem being naked in his presence. But the idea of naked skin on my furniture does not please me. I don't want to spend an afternoon after a lazy morning disinfecting all the surfaces of the house.

I wave him away before stepping into the bathroom. I go through my morning routine in quick tempo. I'm curious what Eli will cook. Can he actually cook? Or is cooking the same as his poker playing? Mediocre at best.

I sniff as I walk toward the kitchen. I smell bacon and potatoes. My stomach rumbles in response to the enticing scents.

I enter the kitchen and nearly stumble to a halt at the sight. Eli is bent over removing a tray from the oven. His back flexes with his movements. He must spend a considerable amount of time in his home gym to create such muscle definition.

My belly warms as I watch him pivot to place the tray on the counter. His ab muscles are a masterpiece.

It's a joy to have Eli in my kitchen. The thought startles me. I don't usually enjoy people in my space. It's why I've never had a roommate – not even in college when it was practically mandatory.

Is this what love is? Wanting another person in your space? Enjoying the sight of them moving around your kitchen?

"Hey," Eli greets when he notices me. "I hope you like bacon and potatoes."

I step closer. "What kind of potatoes?"

"Spicy hash browns. I used to make these by the bucketload for my brothers. You can't believe how much teenage boys eat."

"They smell delicious."

"Thank you. Grab the plates. It's ready." I reach above him to get plates from the cupboard but he nods toward the table. "I already set the table."

I freeze. He went through my cupboards to find dishes? I brace myself for the panic. I count to five but no panic arrives. Huh. Apparently, I don't mind people in my space. As long as the person is Eli.

He plates our food and we settle at the table in the kitchen nook.

"Thanks for cooking. I'm feeling peckish."

He nods to the food. "Go ahead. I promise I didn't poison you. I've only poisoned one person."

I still with my fork poised in front of my mouth. "You poisoned someone?"

He waves away my concern. "It was a mistake. I didn't realize Kai handed me the bottle of expired milk. Miles vomited all day after drinking a glass of the milk."

I grimace. "Did he not realize the milk was sour?"

"Miles hates milk. But I made him drink one glass a day anyway. He held his nose and drank it in one go."

"Mr. Controlling strikes again," I mutter before trying the hash browns. My eyes widen when the taste explodes in my mouth. "These are good."

"You don't have to sound surprised."

"After you poisoned Miles, I'm entitled to be surprised."

"Miles hasn't drunk a glass of milk since then. He dry heaves if he watches someone drink milk." I smirk. "We drink a lot of milk at the holidays."

"You're cruel."

"The milk was a mistake. Unlike when Miles rubbed poison ivy all over my hands while I was sleeping. I had to wear gloves inside for a month."

"You probably deserved it."

Eli shakes a piece of bacon at me. "You're as cruel as my brothers."

I roll my eyes. "You deserved the red dye explosion."

"And the beer in my lap?"

"Deserved as well," I say before digging into my food.

"What do you want to do this morning?" I ask once we've finished eating.

"It's a lazy morning. We can laze on the sofa and read the newspaper or watch a movie or we could crawl back into bed and work off all the calories from this breakfast." He waggles. "I know which option has my preference."

"We need to clean up the kitchen first."

Eli stands. "I've got it."

"But you cooked."

"I want to spoil you. Why don't you grab your Kindle and read while I clean? Maybe read a sexy scene to get you in the mood?"

"I'm not Maya. I don't read romance."

He sighs. "Bummer. I thought we could act out some of the racier scenes."

"You know entirely too much about this."

"I took a women's literature class in college. It was eye opening."

He stands and I start to gather the dishes. He knocks my hands away. "Relax, Lace. Pretend I'm your man servant for the day."

"Does my man servant provide orgasms?"

"Multiple orgasms." He winks.

I laugh as he walks to the sink with the dishes.

My heart warms as I watch him putter in the kitchen. I don't need to question it further. This is love.

I love Eli. The man I can laugh and joke with. The man who brings me unbelievable pleasure in bed. The man who cooks for me. The man I don't mind being in my space.

The man I want to spend the rest of my life with.

Chapter 27

"I didn't think this through." ~ Eli

Eli

Paisley opens her door and I drink her in. I thought the dress she wore to the fundraiser couldn't be topped. I was wrong.

The deep V of this dress dips to her waist revealing a tantalizing trail of naked skin. While the skirt of the dress is loose and flowing, it also has a slit that reaches past her hip.

There is no way she's wearing a bra or panties underneath this dress. I growl. "Tell me you're wearing underwear under this dress."

She blinks. "I'm wearing underwear under this dress."

She's clearly lying. My cock hardens and lengthens as I imagine removing her dress and revealing her naked body. She can keep those sexy stilettos on, though. The gouges they'll cause in my back will be worth it.

"You're lying."

"You made me."

"Are you trying to torture me?"

I wrap an arm around her to draw her near but pause when I touch bare skin. I whirl her around to investigate. Her back is completely bare. My cock pulses in my pants. I want to lavish kisses on her back while I pound into her from behind.

Paisley bats her eyelashes. "Do you not approve of my dress?"

"I'm going to spend the evening fighting off men."

She snorts. "This is Smuggler's Hideaway. The men on this island have ignored me for the past ten years. I think you're good."

"What about the tourists?"

"Tonight is the dance to announce the sexiest man on the island. The tourists are mostly women." She rakes her gaze over me. "I'm the one who'll be spending the evening fighting off women."

I run a hand down my front. "You approve of my tux?"

She shrugs. "It's a bit over the top. Most men wear suits. Some men wear shorts and flip-flops."

"I don't mind sticking out." I wink.

She nods to my hard cock. "You're sticking out now."

"It's your fault."

"You growled those words but I believe it's a compliment."

Honk! Honk!

Paisley glances around me. "This limo is even larger than the last one. If I didn't know any better, I'd say you're trying to compensate for a shorter size elsewhere."

I wrap my arms around her and pull her near – making sure to press my hard length against her. "You can feel I don't have to compensate."

"Which is what I said." She smiles and her hazel eyes sparkle with joy.

My gaze catches on those pretty pink lips. They're currently painted a deep red to match her dress.

"How mad will you be if I destroy your lipstick?"

Her breath hitches. "Lipstick can be repaired."

At her invitation, I press my lips to hers. She tastes of strawberries today – probably from her lipstick – but her exotic taste can't be masked. I moan and thrust my tongue into her mouth.

"If you're going to have sex, we're going on without you!" Chloe shouts and Paisley yanks away from me.

"Why is…" She trails off when Sophia waves at her from where she's sticking out of the sunroof of the limo. "Did you invite all of my friends?"

"I could hardly invite Chloe and Sophia without Nova and Maya."

"Thus, the supersized limo."

"We could do as Chloe suggests. Go inside and have sex while they go to the party." I wiggle my eyebrows.

She bites her bottom lip as she contemplates my question. "Are you serious?"

I was joking but now I'm not. I grasp her hand and start to maneuver her inside. She refuses to budge.

"I haven't missed an end of the summer party on Smuggler's Hideaway since I returned from college. I'm not about to miss one to have sex with you."

"I'll make it worth your while."

She kisses my nose. "You'll make it worth my while when we return home from the party."

I shrug. It was worth a try. I offer her my elbow. "Ready?"

She threads her arm through mine and I guide her down the sidewalk to the limo. The door flies open before we get there.

"You owe me ten bucks," Sophia says.

"If you bet I'd skip the party to have sex with Eli, it's your own fault," Paisley tells her.

"You were practically glued to each other. I thought it was a sure thing."

"Speaking of glued to each other." Nova points to her mouth. "Your lipstick needs refreshing. Both of you."

Smug satisfaction fills me. I love wearing proof Paisley can't keep her hands off of me.

We settle in the limo and the driver starts toward the party.

"I'm glad you nabbed a billionaire. I've never been in a limo before. There's a bar." Chloe pops open the refrigerator. "Who wants a shot of whiskey?"

Maya shakes her head. "No thanks."

"Are you feeling nauseous?" Paisley asks.

Caleb scowls. "She's always feeling nauseous. We should have stayed home."

Maya glares at him. "I'm pregnant. I'm perfectly capable of making my own decisions."

He sighs. "It's hard to watch the person I can't live without throw up multiple times a day."

Maya softens. "It'll get better in the second trimester."

"In the meantime." Paisley hands her a candy. "Ginger will help."

Maya pops the candy in her mouth. "Thanks."

"I'll take one," Chloe says.

"Is there something you need to tell me, Wildcat?" Lucas asks.

She pats his chest. "I'm not pregnant. But I want to try ginger candy for nausea due to a hangover."

"Are you planning on having a hangover?"

She shrugs. "I don't plan on them. They just happen. It's inexplicable."

He nods to the whiskey. "Hard to figure out why you have hangovers."

Chloe lifts the bottle into the air. "Who's in for shots?"

Nova raises her hand. "I am."

Hudson growls, "Sunshine."

She shoves her palm in his face. "Don't you dare sunshine me. I pumped all day today so I could drink tonight."

"Did you mark the breast milk this time?"

"Stop being a baby. You're not going to die because you drank some of my breast milk."

Sophia barks out a laugh. "I need to hear this story."

The limo comes to a stop in front of the entrance to *Hideaway Haven Resort.*

"Did you sponsor the party?" I ask Hudson as we exit the limo since he owns the resort.

He grunts in response.

"Grunting is a yes by the way," Nova says.

I grasp Paisley's hand. "In case I forgot to tell you, you look beautiful tonight."

Her cheeks flush. "Thank you."

I squeeze her hand. "Is everyone ready?" I ask the group before leading them inside the resort and to the ballroom.

The ballroom is decorated in true Smuggler's Hideaway style. The tables are covered in shimmering blue, teal, and iridescent tablecloths to mimic ocean waves. Pearls, driftwood, and seashells serve as centerpieces. Old whiskey barrels, mini wooden crates filled with vintage-style rum bottles, and antique lanterns are scattered around the room. Nautical fishing nets have been draped over the ceiling and intertwined with twinkle lights.

"The mayor is making a beeline toward us. I'm getting a drink." Flynn hurries away.

"You don't have to be afraid of her. She doesn't actually want to be in a polyamorous relationship with you. She's teasing you," Sophia shouts as she chases him.

The rest of our friends hurry after them. I wait for the mayor since *Buccaneer's Whiskey* is sponsoring the event.

"Good," Lana says when she reaches us. "You're here."

"How can I help?" Assuming I can help, I left most of the arrangements for the sponsorship with my assistant. I scan the crowd but I don't see Dakota anywhere.

"I need you backstage."

My brow furrows. "Backstage?"

"It's where the finalists wait until the results of the election are announced."

"I didn't agree to announce the winners."

"Don't be silly. You're not announcing. You are the winner." Her eyes widen and she steps closer. "Sorry. The winner is supposed to be top secret."

Paisley tries to tug her hand from mine. "I'll join my friends."

I tighten my hold to stop her from escaping. "You're not going anywhere because I'm not doing this."

Lana huffs. "But you were voted the sexiest man on the island."

"I don't give a shit."

She motions to the room. "Why did you sponsor all of this if you're going to ruin the event?"

"I'm not ruining the event. I'm merely refusing to participate."

The finalists in the sexiest man on the island competition are auctioned off to the highest bidder. The prize is a date with the finalist. No way am I going on a date with any other woman than Paisley. And I refuse to be auctioned off like a piece of meat.

"But then we'll be short one man. The proceeds of the auction are important for the town."

"Send me an invoice. I'll pay for whatever Smuggler's Rest needs but I won't be auctioned off."

"It's a good cause," Paisley says.

"Do you want me to go out on a date with another woman?"

"No, but maybe I'll win the auction."

"And maybe your sister will win."

She recoils and I immediately regret my words. "I'm sorry. I'm an asshole."

"It's okay."

I palm her neck and squeeze. "No, it's not. Considering what happened with your ex and Darcy, I should know better. I'm sorry."

I touch my lips to hers. The kiss is entirely too brief. But I'm weak when it comes to her. If I meld my lips to hers, I'll be banging her in the women's restroom in no time.

Lana sighs. "I love love. I can't cause an issue between young lovers. I'll find a replacement."

She bustles away and I blow out a breath. "I thought you were going to have to sneak me out of here for a minute there."

Paisley smiles. "You didn't but I'd sneak you out."

"Will you hide me under your dress?" I waggle my eyebrows.

"You're a bad boy, Eli Raider."

"I'm your bad boy."

"And my sister isn't stealing you away."

"No one's stealing me away."

Because Paisley is mine. Maybe not forever. But for as long as she stays, she's mine.

Chapter 28

PAISLEY

"Ugh," Chloe groans. "I'm still hungover from the end of the summer ball."

I frown at her. "The ball was several days ago. You shouldn't still be hungover."

"I am. And it's your fault."

I rear back. "Why is it my fault?"

"Your boyfriend filled the limo's bar with whiskey."

I lift an eyebrow. "And then he forced the liquid down your throat?"

She nods. "Exactly."

"And you didn't dare his brother, Kai, that you could drink more shots than him?"

"He started it," she pouts.

"Because our Chloe never starts shit," Sophia says.

"It's true. I'm a reformed woman."

At Chloe's proclamation, I burst into laughter with the rest of my friends. Chloe may be married and have a stepdaughter she dotes on now but she will never be reformed.

She throws a coaster at me. "I'm being serious."

Maya rubs her still flat stomach. "Try being pregnant."

Nova nods in agreement. "I'd take a whiskey hangover over morning sickness any day of the week."

"But then you wouldn't have little Iliana," Sophia points out.

Nova smiles. "True. She loves Hudson more than me and she can scream for hours on end without reason, but I love the little terror."

Maya sighs. "I can't wait to have my own terror."

"I hope you have a boy. Iliana can fall in love with him and then we'll be a family for real."

Maya squeezes her hand. "We are a family for real."

My heart fills with joy for Maya. She longed for her parents to love her for most of her life. Until Caleb showed her what true love is. Now she no longer puts up with shit from her parents.

"Hey!" Chloe slaps a hand on the table. "I have a daughter, too. Maybe she'll fall in love with Maya's son."

Maya frowns. "It would be quite the age difference. Natalia's thirteen now."

"Fine. I'll get pregnant and my son will fall in love with Iliana."

"What if you have a girl?" Nova asks.

"Then, *she* will fall in love with Iliana."

Sophia claps her hands. "I think we're getting off track here. We're supposed to be discussing the financial situation of *Five Fathoms Brewing*."

"Does Flynn have any idea when he'll be able to finish the repairs on the brewery?" I ask.

"We'll still waiting for the insurance company to process our claim," Maya answers.

"I thought we agreed to begin the repairs immediately."

"No." Nova shakes her head. "We agreed to wait once Eli offered us space for the brewery at his distillery."

I fidget in my seat. "I'm uncomfortable accepting handouts from Eli."

Sophia waves away my concern. "He's a billionaire. He can afford it."

I narrow my eyes on her. "It's wrong to take advantage of him just because he's wealthy."

She lifts an eyebrow. "But we can take advantage of him because he's your boyfriend?"

"No."

"No, he's not your boyfriend?"

"What are you? Ten?"

"I love this," Nova says.

My brow wrinkles. "You love how immature Sophia's being?"

"I love how you've fallen in love. How we've all fallen in love."

"And," Maya adds, "we're all staying on the island."

Nova smiles. "Our kids are going to be best friends."

I hold up a hand. "I'm not certain I want children."

"Why not?" Nova asks.

Chloe moans. "You had to ask? She's going to start lecturing us on the state of the world and how she's unsure if she should bring children into this messed up world."

"I don't constantly lecture you," I claim.

Chloe raises an eyebrow. "You spent fifteen minutes explaining the difference between paper towels and hand dryers in the restroom at the ball."

"I did not."

"I timed you."

"Really? You timed me? As I recall, you'd lost your shoes and purse by this point of the evening."

She throws her arms in the air. "Then, why did you lecture me?"

I shrug. "Because I could."

She points at me. "You're cruel."

"I'm cruel? I'm not the one who stole the last piece of chocolate cake."

"I didn't want you to bloat in your dress. You were showing a lot of skin."

"It was a sexy dress." Maya sighs. "I bet Eli couldn't wait to tear it off of you when you got home."

He didn't tear it off of me. He lifted the skirt up and had his way with me. It was fantastic. I press my legs together as memories of the night assail my mind. Eli appears all prim and proper in his three-piece suits but the man becomes a bad boy in the bedroom.

Chloe plants her elbows on the table and leans forward. "I want details of whatever has your cheeks turning red."

"I don't need details. I have an excellent imagination."

Chloe rolls her eyes at Maya. "Not all of us inhale romance books faster than a mermaid can swim."

"Speaking of Eli," I begin.

Sophia rubs her hands together. "I can't wait. I bet underneath those suits he's a tiger in bed. Am I right? Wait. Don't tell me. I don't want to be disappointed."

"You're engaged."

She blinks at me. "I don't understand your comment."

"Why do you need details of my sex life when you have a sex life of your own?" I ask.

Her nose wrinkles. "I'm still not understanding your point."

I sigh. "Never mind."

Chloe motions toward me. "Come on. I'm awaiting the details."

"I'm not giving you any details." She pouts. "I want to run something by you."

"If it's whether you should try handcuffs in bed, the answer is yes. The answer is always yes."

My nose wrinkles. "Don't your wrists get sore?"

She shakes her head. "You can't use real handcuffs. You need the fluffy ones. Or you can use scarves as ties. Or ropes. Or—"

I hold up my hand to stop her. "I need to return to the brewery soon. I don't have time to discuss your sexual habits."

"Bummer."

"What were you going to say about Eli?" Maya asks.

"I want to have a surprise birthday party for him. But—"

"Yes!" Nova pumps her arm. "What a great idea. We can host it at the resort. I'll phone Hudson and ask when there's availability."

She whips out her phone but I snatch it from her before she can dial.

"Wait. There's more."

Chloe leans in closer. "More? Do you want to have a sex party? I've never been to one. What does it entail? Do I have to participate or can I watch? Is everyone naked?"

I stare at her with wide eyes. "Where did you get the idea I want to have a sex party?"

She shrugs. "You enjoyed orgy porn when we were teenagers."

I groan. I am never going to hear the end of that.

"Hudson is not going to agree to a sex party," Nova says. "He's very protective of me. He won't want anyone seeing me naked."

"Same for Caleb," Maya adds. "And he won't go naked either. I haven't managed to get him to go swimming in shorts yet. He's very sensitive about the scarring on his leg. Naked is a no go."

"I doubt Flynn would go for it either. I'm sorry, Paisley, but I can't attend," Sophia says.

"I am not having a sex party!" I shout since my friends apparently can't hear me when I speak in a normal voice at a reasonable level.

"We'll figure something else out," Chloe says. "Maybe a costume party."

"Will everyone please quiet down and listen to me for one minute?" I grumble. I don't wait for them to agree before continuing, "Eli never celebrates his birthday. His family has this tradition of doing full day celebrations but Eli never participates."

"Sad. Why not?" Nova asks.

I don't answer her question. If she doesn't remember Eli's dad leaving the week before his sixteenth birthday, it's best not to remind her. Eli doesn't want anyone to pity him.

"I want to do something fun for him. He's always doing everything for me. I want to be the one to surprise him this time."

Sophia nods. "Then, we're doing this."

"We'll help you plan. We know planning a party isn't your strong suit," Nova says.

"I don't want Eli to find out. No one can tell him." My friends nod but it's not good enough for me. "Mermaid pinky promise."

I personally don't believe in mermaids but my friends take mermaid pinky promises seriously. We link our pinkies together. "No one will tell Eli."

"Promise," they say in unison.

"This is going to be so much fun," Chloe squeals.

Maya flips a page in her notebook. "What's your budget?"

"Budget?" I didn't think about a budget. "I thought we'd invite everyone to the bar and then yell surprise when Eli walks in."

Sophia bursts into laughter. "You're cute."

"We need a theme." Chloe drums her fingers on the table. "I'm thinking rumrunners."

"What about a prohibition era speakeasy on the sea?" Sophia suggests.

"Or pirate smugglers' hideout? We could do a treasure hunt, pirate-themed trivia, and a rum-tasting bar," Nova says.

"What about an island of the lost legends theme? We could have a storytelling circle, a solve the mystery game, and a hidden speakeasy," Maya adds.

I moan. "I'm not getting away with a party at the bar, am I?"

Maya pats my hand. "It'll be fun. I promise."

"Do you think Eli will enjoy it?" I ask because his happiness is all that matters.

I want Eli to be happy. I love him. His happiness is the most important thing to me.

I should probably tell him I love him at some point. But the time is never right. It's a terrible excuse but what if he doesn't feel the same? What if he runs away? What if he ends us?

I rub my chest as pain blooms. I can't chance it. Not yet.

Chapter 29

"I heard what I heard." ~ Eli

ELI

I don't want Eli to find out. No one can tell him. Paisley's words have been on repeat in my mind for the past day.

I ignore the light in Paisley's office as I march into the office building of *Buccaneer's Whiskey*. The same way I've been ignoring her for the past day.

I went to *Five Fathoms* to surprise her and take her out for dinner. Instead, I walked in on her having a meeting with her friends about me. *No one can tell him.*

Fucking secrets. I hate secrets. I knew better than to trust anyone but I went ahead and fell for Paisley anyway. Or, rather, the version of Paisley she showed me. I obviously don't know the real woman.

"Good morning," Dakota calls as I walk past her desk.

I grunt in response.

"What crawled up your ass? You're grumpier than Mr. High and Mighty."

"None of your business," I grumble.

Rhett exits his office and stands in front of me with his arms crossed over his chest. "You don't speak to Dakota that way."

I rub a hand down my face. I shouldn't take my frustration with women out on my assistant. "Sorry, Dakota."

She waves my apology away. "No reason to apologize to me just because Mr. High and Mighty ordered it."

"Stop calling me Mr. High and Mighty," Rhett orders Dakota.

"Stop acting all high and mighty and I might consider it."

I don't have time for their antics today. I have things to arrange. I motion for Rhett to move out of my way. He steps to the side but then follows me into my office and shuts the door behind him.

"What's wrong?" I ask as I settle behind my desk.

"That's my question."

"Nothing's wrong," I lie. "Just busy."

"You're always busy, but you're usually not an asshole."

"I apologized for barking at Dakota."

"You've been an asshole since yesterday."

"Only since yesterday? I'm falling down on the job." I chuckle but it's forced.

"What's going on with you? Is there a problem with the distillery? Or *Apparoo*?"

There isn't but I latch onto the excuse. "I need to visit *Apparoo*. I'll probably be gone for a few weeks."

"A few weeks? I thought you were done traveling back and forth between Smuggler's Hideaway and California."

I thought I was, too. I also thought I could trust Paisley. Apparently, I don't know shit.

I feign nonchalance. "It's only a few weeks."

Maybe longer if I can get away with it. I don't want to spend time on this island where Paisley is running around keeping secrets from me. I've had enough of people keeping secrets from me.

Dad left a week before my sixteenth birthday but his departure wasn't sudden. He'd planned it in detail. He had an apartment already rented in another state. And a woman waiting for him there.

I was blindsided by his betrayal. I refuse to be blindsided ever again.

"I can't neglect my role at *Apparoo*."

Rhett frowns. "I didn't say you were."

"Good. If there's nothing else?"

"What the hell is going on with you?"

"I already answered this question. I'm busy and need to travel to California. I have a lot on my plate."

"Unlike me?"

"I'm not comparing us."

He raises his eyebrows. "You're not?"

The door flies open and Paisley marches inside.

I glare at Rhett. "I thought you locked the door."

"Good luck." He pats Paisley on the shoulder. "Maybe you can straighten him out."

I wait until he leaves before addressing Paisley, "Can I help you?"

She rears back. "Can you help me?"

"Yes." I nod. "This is a work environment. I'm the CEO. What can I do for you?"

"It never bothered you about how this was a work environment before."

Visions of taking her on the sofa in her office try to invade my mind but I shove them away. There will be no repeats of the event. In fact, there will be no sex with Paisley whatsoever. I can't be with someone I don't trust.

"That was before."

"Before what? What crawled up your ass and died? I warned you my friends wouldn't behave at the ball. There are a limited amount of times I can apologize for Chloe daring your brothers to go skinny dipping in the resort's swimming pool."

"I don't give a shit what your friends do."

Her nose wrinkles in confusion. I refuse to think it's cute. There's nothing cute about Paisley the liar. "Then, what's wrong?"

"You seriously have to ask?"

"Obviously since I'm asking now."

"I can't believe you."

"I'm beyond confused and I hate being confused. Can you please explain yourself?"

"You need me to explain myself?"

"Yes."

"Fine." I snarl. "I'll explain myself." I lean forward and hiss toward her. "I heard you."

"Heard me what? Yell at my assistant?" Her cheeks darken. "I know it was wrong of me to raise my voice at Blossom. I lost my temper. It won't happen again."

"What the hell are you talking about?"

"I'm discussing your anger at me for raising my voice at my assistant. Although it's not any of your business, the brewery is technically on the distillery's property so I can understand your concern with how I acted."

Is she really this clueless? Or is she making shit up? Are these more lies?

"I realize I'm a hypocrite. I yelled at Blossom for making out with someone at work. Considering what we did in my office, it's beyond hypocritical. But I was shocked at what I saw. I never want to see Jaxon's naked rear end again."

"Jaxon and Blossom were having sex in the distillery?"

Her brow wrinkles. "Technically they were still on the fore-play stage but yes."

"Whatever. Jaxon's a grown man he can do what he wants."

"If you're not mad about Jaxon, what are you mad about?"

"I told you. I heard you."

"What exactly did you hear?"

"You said – and I quote here – Eli can't find out."

Her eyes widen. "You heard?"

"And now I know you're a liar."

Her brow wrinkles. "A liar?"

"Yes. A liar. A woman I can't trust." I shake my head. "I thought you were different. I thought I could trust you. Hell, I thought I…" I trail off before I tell her I thought I loved her.

I don't want her to have an excuse to try and dig her way back into my good graces.

All this time I thought she didn't care about my money. She certainly fooled me.

"You're taking my words out of context."

"I don't know what context could be good."

"Listen, I'm—"

I hold up my hand. "I don't want to hear any more lies. I don't want to hear anything more from you at all."

Her eyes narrow on me. "Are you serious? You heard something out of context and now you're throwing away what we have?"

"We had nothing. It was just a bit of fun. Nothing more."

Pain flashes in her eyes. "Just a bit of fun?"

"Yep. And I did have fun. But now it's over."

She sniffs and tears well in her eyes, but I refuse to be moved by her act. And it is an act. It's been an act all along. What was I thinking? Pursuing her? She planned the entire thing. She lured me in and I fell for it. Hook, line, and sinker. I'm a fucking idiot.

"You're breaking up with me?"

"We're done."

The tears fall from her eyes and I lock my limbs before I go to her. It's a lie, I remind myself. It's all a lie. It's not real. It's a mirage. She isn't the woman I thought she was.

She rushes from the room and I blow out a breath. It's done. I don't need to see Paisley ever again.

Dakota stomps into my office. "You're worse than your brother. You're an asshole. I'm taking a mental health day because I can't look at you right now."

"You don't know what she did."

She throws daggers at me from her eyes. "Neither do you, asshole."

"What do you know?"

"I know you're an asshole who will never deserve Paisley." She shakes her head. "After everything she's been through with her family and her asshole ex. I expected better of you."

Guilt tries to push its way into my conscious but I ignore it. I refuse to feel guilty for scraping Paisley off. I'm not the one in the wrong. I'm not the one who can't be trusted.

Chapter 30

"Is being left alone too much to ask?" ~ Paisley

PAISLEY

I open the door to discover Maya, Nova, Chloe, and Sophia on my doorstep.

"Will it help if I order you to leave?"

Chloe snorts. "You're cute."

She pushes her way inside. Sophia, Nova, and Maya follow her. Maya squeezes my hand as she passes.

"Who told you?" I ask once they've made themselves comfortable in my living room.

"Blossom phoned me," Nova says.

"And Dakota phoned me," Chloe says.

I groan. "So, basically, every person on the island knows Eli dumped me. Great."

"Dakota said there was a loud shouting match and items were thrown," Chloe claims.

I cross my arms over my chest and glare at her. "No items were thrown."

Although, now I'm thinking about it, I kind of wish I'd thrown something at Eli's big, fat head. It would have been better than running off with tears in my eyes like some lame heroine in one of Maya's romance novels.

"Bummer." Sophia frowns. "Assholes should get what they deserve."

"He's going to be alone for the rest of his life. That's his just desserts," Maya says.

"As much as I'd enjoy imagining Eli alone and lonely in his old age, it's never going to happen. He's a billionaire. Eventually, someone will snap him up."

And they can have him. Eli is dead to me. I never should have let him convince me he isn't an asshole. He had me fooled. And, if there's one thing I hate, it's being fooled.

Chloe taps her chin. "Could we sabotage his wealth somehow?"

Nova frowns at her. "You can't prank his wealth away."

Chloe smiles. "But we could prank him. Rumor has it he's afraid of Viking the otter."

"Viking is adorable," Maya says. "How can anyone be afraid of him?"

"Eli claims Viking bit him." I roll my eyes. "He barely had a scuff on his shoes."

I should have known then to stay away from him. Anyone who can get angry with an innocent little creature, who's adorable to boot, should be avoided. Lesson learned.

No more spending time with Eli. No more early morning coffees at the brewery while everyone else is still asleep. No more surprise trips. No more dates where Eli spends the entire time teasing me with what he'll do to me later. And no more nights spent in his arms.

"I'm going to die alone."

Nova rushes to me and engulfs me in a hug. "You're not going to die alone."

Maya rubs a hand up and down my back. "This is just a bump in the road. Eli will realize his mistake and come crawling back."

I step away from them. "No. There will be no reconciliation with Eli. And you're not going to spend the day convincing me otherwise."

"Good." Sophia rubs her hands together. "We can get to the fun portion of our evening. We can—"

"figure out how to prank Eli," Chloe interrupts to say.

"No. We are not pranking Eli."

Chloe sticks out her bottom lip. "Why not?"

"There's no sense in pranking him anyway," Nova says before I can explain my aversion to spending time in jail – again. "According to Blossom, Eli's leaving today and he won't be back for at least a few weeks."

My stomach cramps. He's leaving. He dumped me and is leaving? He doesn't even want to try and reconcile? He's avoiding me as if he's disgusted with me?

I place a hand on my stomach and force those thoughts away. I don't want to reconcile with Eli. He's a First Class Douchebag who couldn't even be bothered to listen to my side of the story.

I can't be with a man who won't listen to me. I spent my childhood with a stepfather and mother who didn't care about my thoughts or feelings. I won't spend a lifetime with a partner who does the same.

"If we're not pranking him, can we at least get drunk?" Chloe asks.

"I'm pregnant," Maya says.

"Breastfeeding," Nova adds.

"All the more for us." Chloe walks toward the door.

"Have a good time," I holler after her.

She points at me. "You're coming with."

"No, I am not. I am not going to Mermaid Karaoke and singing my heart out."

She shrugs. "Summer's over. Mermaid Karaoke is done anyway."

"And I am not going to *Rumrunner* and drinking shots of whiskey all night."

"But *Rumrunner* and *Bootlegger* are the only bars in Smuggler's Rest," she pouts.

"We could go to the resort," Sophia suggests. "Or to *Smuggler's Cove*."

"No way." Nova shakes her head. "I'm not getting banned from the restaurant because you three got drunk and rowdy at the bar."

"I didn't say anything about getting rowdy," Chloe says.

Nova rolls her eyes. "It's implied."

"Fine. We'll go to the resort." Chloe motions to the door. "Let's load up!"

Not happening. "I'm not going to the resort."

Chloe huffs. "What's the problem now? We won't get banned from there. Nova's baby daddy owns the place."

Nova glares at her. "Stop referring to Hudson as my baby daddy."

"Why? Is he not Iliana's dad?" Chloe feigns confusion. She's lying. She's also being a good friend. She's trying to take my mind off of Eli. It's sweet. But it's not going to work.

"I don't feel like going anywhere," I say before collapsing in a chair. "Go have fun. I'll see you later."

"She's cute," Sophia says. "She actually thinks we'll leave her alone."

I don't. But it was worth a try.

"No worries. I'll grab the supplies." Chloe flounces out of my house.

"Supplies?" I ask the room but no one will meet my gaze. Not a good sign with my friends who aren't exactly known for their ability to follow the rules.

"You sit there." Nova pats my shoulder. "We'll take care of everything."

Scarier words have never been spoken.

"I'll get the glasses." Sophia hurries to the kitchen.

"Don't forget plates," Maya hollers after her. She pats her belly. "Mini Caleb's hungry."

"Mini Caleb?" Nova asks. "You know you're having a boy?"

Maya shakes her head. "No idea but there's no way Caleb's super powered genes haven't overpowered mine."

Nova nods. "I know what you mean. Iliana is a girl but she's all Hudson. She points to stuff and grunts at it."

"I'm back," Chloe sings as she barges into the house.

And there goes any hope I had of my friends leaving me to suffer on my own. Chloe has snacks and drinks. She'll never leave now.

I bet I could construct a wild child signal. I could flash it in the air whenever Chloe gets out of control and Lucas would rush in to snatch her away. It's an idea worth considering.

Chloe slams a bottle of whiskey on the table. "It's truth or drink time."

I groan. There's no way I'm surviving this night unscathed. I should probably phone Blossom and tell her I'll be in late tomorrow.

Nova pats my arm. "Don't worry. I already told Blossom you won't be in tomorrow."

Damn. There went my last excuse to get out of this situation. Oh, wait. I have another idea.

"But Nova and Maya can't play truth or drink."

Chloe smirks. "Yes, they can. If they have to drink, they have to drink a glass of prune juice."

Nova moans. "I hate prune juice. Hudson made me drink it all the time when I was pregnant since it's good for hydration."

"Don't tell Caleb. I have no interest in downing gallons of prune juice. It's disgusting." Maya makes a face.

"Any more excuses?" Sophia asks as she sets out plates and glasses.

"I believe the game is truth or dare. Not truth or drink."

She shakes her head. "Lame. I expected more of you."

Chloe sets a charcuterie board on the table. My mouth actually waters at the sight of the various cheeses and meats and nuts.

"Did you make this?"

"Don't sound so surprised. I can cook."

Sophia barks out a laugh. "No, you can't."

Chloe huffs. "Fine. Natalia helped me. She's a whizz in the kitchen. She doesn't take after me."

Maya fills up a plate with meats and cheeses and hands it to me. "Eat. You're going to need it."

My stomach rumbles at the scent of food. I can't remember when I last ate. Probably breakfast. Oh, wait. I didn't have breakfast since Eli normally brings me a muffin in the morning. But not this morning. This morning he...

I stuff a piece of Gouda in my mouth and force those thoughts away. No more thinking about Eli the First Degree Jerk.

Chloe pours whiskey into three shot glasses and hands one to me. "You're first."

I sigh. Of course, I am. I don't fight her. I've resigned myself to the hangover I'll be feeling for at least two days after tonight.

"Ask your question."

Sophia opens her mouth but Chloe shoves her palm in her face. "Me first." She smirks at me. "Did Eli have a big dick?"

And so, it begins. I down the shot.

"Darn," Chloe pouts in disappointment but Sophia elbows her.

"Do you want her passed out drunk or do you want to know how big Eli is?"

Chloe blinks. "Why can't I want both things?"

I narrow my eyes on Sophia. "You want me passed out drunk?"

"I want you to forget about Eli and what happened today for a little while. And, since you have a brain that never stops thinking, there's only one way for you to forget what happened."

Huh. Her motives are actually kind of sweet.

"Nova." Chloe hands her a glass of prune juice. "You're next."

"I get to ask a question this time," Sophia says and Nova groans. "Did you or did you not know you could escape the chalet the night you got 'locked in' with Hudson and created Iliana?"

"I hope you have extra toilet paper in the house," Nova mutters as she drinks the glass of prune juice.

I bark out a laugh. I didn't think it would be possible to laugh today. But I should have known better. I should have known my friends wouldn't let me sit alone in my house with my broken heart. They never let me down. I can always count on them.

No matter what happens in life. I have them.

Chapter 31

"So much for airport security." ~ Eli

ELI

Caleb steps onto my plane and whistles. "Wow. This is fancy."

Flynn scans the interior. "Is this standard? Or do you get to customize the interior?"

Hudson sits across from me. He caresses the leather seat. "I've traveled in private jets, but I don't think I'd like to own one."

Lucas and Flynn sit on either side of him while Caleb sits next to me.

"What are you doing here?" I ask them.

"I don't know about them, but I'm here to kick your ass," Caleb says.

"I'm here to watch," Hudson says.

"I'm here to make sure no one gets arrested," Lucas says.

"I'm here to tell you what an asshole you are," Flynn says.

Caleb looks at him. "Do you tell him what an asshole he is before I kick his ass?"

Flynn shrugs. "I don't mind. You can go first."

Caleb cracks his knuckles. "Awesome. I have a lot of pent up aggression."

Hudson nods. "Did they make Maya drink a gallon of prune juice, too?"

"Yep. She spent the night in the bathroom." Caleb smirks at me. "She promised I could kick your ass as punishment."

I hold up my hands. "It's not my fault Maya drank a gallon of prune juice."

Caleb glares at me. "It sure as hell is."

I run a hand down my face. "Help a smuggler out. Tell me what's going on."

Flynn lifts an eyebrow. "You're a smuggler? You're not running away like a little bitch?"

I growl. "I'm not a little bitch."

"Then, you're not running away?"

"I need to be in California for a few weeks."

Lucas crosses his arms over his chest and leans back into his seat. "Funny how your assistant, Dakota, claims this trip was sudden and she never planned any meetings for you."

"You can't blame me for wanting a break."

"We can't?" Hudson asks.

"Wouldn't you want a break from Smuggler's Hideaway if you discovered Nova was a liar who you couldn't trust?"

He growls. "Caleb, I'm usurping you. I'm kicking his ass."

Caleb shakes his head. "I called dibs on the way here."

The pilot steps out of the cockpit. "Sir, would you like to delay your departure?"

"If he knows what's good for him, he won't be departing at all," Hudson grumbles.

"I need a few minutes," I tell the pilot.

He nods and returns to the cockpit.

Caleb smiles. "It's good you recognize how quickly I can kick your ass."

"You're ex-military—"

He growls. "Former military."

"Former military," I correct. "I keep in shape but I know my limitations."

"Question." Flynn raises his hand. "Does knowing his limitations mean he understands he's an asshole?"

Lucas taps his cheek. "I don't think so."

"Do we explain what an asshole he is before or after Hudson and Caleb tear him into pieces?"

Lucas sighs. "No tearing from limb to limb. I can't explain away bloodshed."

"But you said we could beat him up," Caleb practically pouts.

"Knock him around, give him a few bruises, but no bloodshed."

"What about broken bones? I promise they won't be compound fractures." Caleb rakes his gaze over me.

I lock my muscles before I squirm in my seat. Guessing by the anger flaring in his eyes, Caleb is dead serious.

"You can't beat me up because I broke up with Paisley," I argue.

"Yes, we can," Hudson says.

"It'll be my pleasure."

I admit it. Caleb is now officially scaring the fuck out of me.

"If we had known you wouldn't treat Paisley with kid gloves, we would have never let you near her," Flynn says. "Not after the way the wicked stepsisters and evil stepdad handled her."

"Don't forget her mom," Hudson adds. "She lets her husband treat her daughter with malice. I will never allow anyone to treat Iliana badly. I'll kill them first."

Lucas sighs. "Can we cut out the talk of killing when I'm around?"

Hudson frowns at him. "You're off duty."

"Have you met my wife? I'm never off duty."

Flynn nods. "It's true. Your wife is a wild child."

Lucas growls. "Not a wild child anymore."

Flynn raises his hands in surrender. "I misspoke. She's a troublemaker, not a wild child."

Lucas grins. "She's a troublemaker all right."

"I still disagree with the use of prune juice," Caleb says.

Lucas shrugs. "Chloe didn't want Maya or Nova to feel left out."

"Maya wouldn't have felt left out. My shy bunny isn't as shy anymore."

Hudson chuckles. "Rumor has it she's the one who suggested leaving Viking the otter in Eli's house."

I squirm in my seat. Viking is out to get me. The otter appears all sweet and cuddly but the second you turn your back, he bites you. He's a mean little furball.

Flynn points to me. "Judging by how scared Eli is, we should have brought Viking with us."

"I'm not scared."

Caleb snorts. "And I'm not eagerly anticipating kicking your ass into the next state."

"I have a plane. I'll be in the next state shortly."

"I guess we better buckle in." Hudson digs for the seatbelt. "I don't mind going for a test ride. I wonder if Nova would want one of these."

"Nah." Flynn shakes his head. "Nova isn't interested in your money."

"Unlike some women," I mutter.

Silence falls and I realize I fucked up.

"Are you saying Paisley was after your money?" Hudson grumbles.

Flynn narrows his eyes on me. "The woman who wouldn't accept a dime from her evil stepfather is a gold digger?"

Caleb rubs his hands together. "Can I hit him now?"

I snarl at him. "You can't hit me because you don't want to accept the truth."

His eyes widen. "Accept the truth? I'm the one who doesn't want to accept the truth?"

"I didn't stutter, did I?"

"You know," Lucas begins, "I don't know if I should feel sorry for him. He's obviously an idiot. Or turn around so you can tear him limb to limb."

Hudson stands. "I vote tear him limb to limb."

Caleb unfolds from his seat and joins him. "Finally. We're getting to the good part."

I face them. I'm not a coward. I'm also in the right. They can beat me up as much as they want. It won't change anything. Paisley is a liar who can't be trusted.

Caleb narrows his eyes as he studies me. "Why does he appear all righteous?"

"Because he's an idiot who still hasn't learned he's wrong," Hudson answers.

"I am not wrong," I seethe. "I heard what I heard."

"Which is why you let Paisley explain what she meant when she confronted you. Like I said. Idiot." Hudson shakes his head.

I fist my hands. "How else am I supposed to interpret *I don't want Eli to find out. No one can tell him* other than Paisley is keeping secrets from me and is not to be trusted?"

"You were right when you said he's an idiot," Flynn mutters.

"Fucking idiot," Lucas adds.

Caleb stabs my chest. "Paisley's planning a surprise birthday party for you. She knows you don't enjoy celebrating your birthday, so she wanted to surprise you. She knew you wouldn't agree to a party."

My mouth falls open. "What?"

Hudson sighs. "Everyone on the island knows your dad left right before your sixteenth birthday."

I flinch.

He squeezes my shoulder. "Paisley wanted to turn a bad memory into a good one."

I study their faces. Are they being serious? No one tries to hide from me or glance away. They all meet my gaze full on.

"Paisley asked her friends for help because she's not much of a party planner," Lucas says.

My feet won't hold me. I collapse in my chair. "I fucked up."

"Does this mean we can't beat him up?" Caleb asks.

"I deserve for you to kick my ass." After the way I treated Paisley, I deserve all the shit they can send my way and more.

Caleb sits next to me. "It's no fun when you accept it."

I run a hand down my face. "What am I going to do?"

"Do you want Paisely?" Lucas asks.

"I love her. She's my whole world."

I've been terrified to say those words. To admit my feelings for Paisley. And my terror led me to lose her.

Crap. I've lost the woman I love. The woman I can't live without. The woman I don't want to live without.

"Let's make a plan to get her back then," Caleb says.

"It's too late. I destroyed her."

He claps me on the shoulder. "If Maya can forgive me for what I did, Paisley will forgive you."

I shake my head. "Maya is sweet and loves you."

"And Paisley loves you."

"She never said."

He snorts. "And you told her how you feel?"

I don't answer since he's right. I've been lying to myself about how much I love her. Naturally, I didn't give her the words she needs to hear.

I drop my face into my hands. "What am I going to do?"

"First, you're going to tell the pilot you're not flying to California," Hudson says.

"Then," Lucas adds, "we're going to figure out a plan."

I cringe. "A grand gesture? I'm not a grand gesture kind of guy."

"Do you want Paisley back or are you going to be a whiney little bitch?" Flynn asks.

I glare at him. I'm not a whiney little bitch. "Fine. But someone else has to come up with the plan."

"No problem." He rubs his hands together. "I'm engaged to Sophia. I've learned a few tricks."

Lucas scoffs. "I'm married to Chloe. I'll take your few tricks and raise you a pocketful of ideas."

While they brainstorm ideas, I stand and walk to the cockpit. There's no way I'm going to California if there's a chance I can win Paisley back.

Paisley. My chest aches and I rub a hand over it. I let my fears guide me. I should have just listened to her when she tried to explain. But I was too scared to hear what I thought the truth was.

No matter. I'm going to win my Lace back and then I'm never letting her go again.

Chapter 32

"Welp. That was unexpected." ~ Paisley

PAISLEY

"I'm really sorry," Nova apologizes on the phone.

"It's not your fault. But why doesn't Hudson have the staff to handle this?"

The last thing I want to be doing is taking down the decorations for Eli's surprise birthday party. The stupid party is the reason he ended our relationship and broke my heart. I rub a hand over the ache in my chest as I walk toward the entrance to *Hideaway Haven Resort.*

The last time I was here was for the end of summer party. I thought I loved Eli before the party but when he refused to be auctioned off because he was afraid my stepsister would win a date with him, I knew it was love.

Too bad Eli didn't feel the same. While I was falling in love, he was having a good time. Asshole.

"He's short staffed since a lot of the staff go on vacation after the summer holidays," Nova says and I jolt. I forgot I was on the telephone with her.

I scowl. This is not like me. I don't forget things. I'm not scatterbrained. I remember all the facts and figures everyone else forgets.

Stupid love. It's better to avoid it. I learned my lesson once but apparently once wasn't enough when it comes to love. I'm now declaring twice is definitely enough. Love is not for me.

"I'm here now," I say as I enter the resort. "I'll handle it."

"I could come help except Iliana has colic."

I'd love her help. Mostly for moral support. But I can't allow her to bring Iliana when her baby girl isn't feeling well. I'm not an asshole, unlike certain male billionaires who shall remain unnamed.

"Stay home with your precious daughter. I've got this under control."

We hang up and I make my way to the ballroom. When Hudson first proposed adding a ballroom to the resort, I scoffed. A ballroom on Smuggler's Hideaway? There was no need. I was wrong. The room is booked months, if not years, in advance.

I step inside the ballroom and glance around. The decorations are similar to the end of summer dance. Except most of the mermaid paraphernalia has been removed since I refuse to pretend mermaids are real.

I shove my phone in my back pocket and grab one of the boxes lined up against the wall. I put it together before starting to shove stuff from the first table into the box.

The door opens behind me. Thank goodness. Hudson found someone to help me after all.

I spin around with a smile on my face but the smile dies when I see who it is.

"Eli." I guess he won't remain unnamed after all.

"Lace."

I grunt and spin back around to march to the next table. Who does he think he is? Calling me Lace? I'm not Lace to him. I was nothing to him. In fact, I drop the box on the ground.

"What the hell are you doing here?"

I'm giving my anger free rein. Eli deserves it.

He holds up his hand. "Can we talk?"

"Now you want to talk? When I tried explaining things to you earlier, you wouldn't listen. But now you suddenly have time? Forget it. I'm done with you."

I bend over to pick up the box but Eli places a hand on my arm to stop me. I jerk away.

"Do not touch me."

"Sorry. I didn't think."

"Let me clear things up for you. You don't touch a woman without her permission. And, in case your tiny little brain is confused, you do not have permission to touch me."

He sighs and runs a hand down his face. "I deserved that."

I snort. "You deserve a lot worse but I don't have time for you today. I have to clean this up and I need to get back to the brewery."

He growls. "I got your check."

"I assumed as much since I asked Dakota to leave it on your desk."

"I don't want your money."

"Really? Did you forget I'm a gold digger? I will not have you running around the island claiming I used you to have somewhere to host the brewery after the hurricane."

"I would never—"

I hold up a hand. "You can stop whatever you're going to say right there. I can't believe anything you claim you will never do again. Because," I lean forward to hiss in his face, "I don't trust you."

Pain flashes in his eyes but I ignore it. He deserves to feel some pain after the things he said to me. He can't cause me pain and remain unscathed. He's lucky I haven't unleashed my prank power on him.

Yet. I haven't unleashed my prank power on him yet. Because after today, the pranking is back on. I'm not holding Chloe back any more. I'm done being a civil adult. No one else is. Why should I be?

"Can I explain?"

I bark out a laugh. "You want me to allow you to explain? Do I need to explain the definition of hypocrite to you?"

"I know the definition. And I know I fit the definition."

"Good." I clap. "Proud of you."

He picks up a box and puts it together.

"What are you doing?"

"If you're not going to listen to me, I'll help you."

"I don't need your help."

"You have it anyway."

"Whatever. Stay on your side of the room and I'll stay on mine."

I stomp off to the furthest corner of the room. I manage to fill an entire box before he speaks again.

"Can I please explain why I was an asshole?"

"At least you realize you're an asshole."

"I'm the world's biggest asshole for hurting you."

"If you expect me to disagree, you'll be waiting a long time."

He chuckles. "I love how you don't beat around the bush. You tell me how it is. It's one of the things I love about you."

I narrow my eyes on him. "You're not allowed to say there are things you love about me after telling me our relationship was only a bit of fun."

"I was hurting and lashed out."

"You were hurting?" I purse my lips. "You overheard something, misunderstood the meaning, and then unleashed your fury on the world. If you were hurting, it was your own damn fault."

"I know." He clears his throat. "Can I show you something?"

I narrow my eyes on him. "What?"

He removes an item from his back pocket and offers it to me. When I hesitate to take it, he waves it at me. "It's a picture. It won't bite."

I step closer and snatch the picture from him before retreating. I look at it and gasp. The man in this picture could be Eli's twin.

"It's my dad. This was taken a few days before my sixteenth birthday."

My heart aches for him. His dad left right before his sixteenth birthday.

"We had a barbeque on the beach to celebrate. The celebration was a week early because Dad had some business to attend to on the day of my birthday. It turns out the business was leaving his wife and six sons for another woman."

"I'm sorry." I offer him the picture.

"This is the only picture of my dad I kept," he murmurs as he stares at the photograph. "Mom wanted no evidence of his existence in the house after he left."

"Weren't her six sons evidence of his existence?"

"Nah. We're her sons. Not their sons."

"Makes sense."

"I never thought I'd see my dad again."

My brow wrinkles. "You've seen him? He hasn't returned to Smuggler's Hideaway." If he had, I'd know about it. The smuggler's grapevine is efficient and thorough.

"He visited me in California. He couldn't find my home address so he showed up at the corporate headquarters for *Apparoo.*"

Despite myself, I'm curious. "Did he want to reconcile?"

Eli snorts. "Nah. He wanted money."

"And now you think everyone wants money from you."

He cringes. "I shouldn't have called you a gold digger."

"There are a lot of things you shouldn't have done." I don't give him an out. If I give him an out now, he'll run all over me in the future. I shake my head. What am I thinking? There is no future with Eli.

"You're correct. And I apologize for all of them. Starting with I should have never told the woman I love that she meant nothing to me."

"No, you shouldn't have. I obviously—" I stop when my brain catches up. "Did you say woman you love?"

He smiles. "I love you, Lace. I've known since the day I met your evil stepsisters and your mom. I couldn't believe how strong you are considering how they tried to beat you down. I knew then you were the woman for me."

"And yet you pushed me away."

"I was scared. I don't trust anyone to stick around. My dad didn't. He planned his departure for months. Unbeknownst to me. I was blindsided."

"I understand your dad left and it sucks. But who else has left you? Your mom worked her fingers to the bone to provide for you and your brothers. Your brothers all stayed on Smuggler's Hideaway. Not one of them left. Your best friend, Jeremy, has stuck by your side. According to you, he doesn't complain about you wanting to live in Smuggler's Hideaway instead of California."

He runs a hand down his face. "You're right."

"Get used to it. I'm always right."

"Does this mean you forgive me?"

How can I not forgive him? He was an idiot but he owned up to his mistakes. It's not easy to admit you're wrong. Plus, I love him.

"I have conditions."

"Name them. Whatever you want."

"One, you cash the check."

He scowls. "You don't owe me for helping you out."

"It's from *Five Fathoms Brewing,* not me personally."

He blows out a breath. "Fine. What else?"

"You have to work on jumping to conclusions when you hear me speak out of context. If you're worried or concerned, you ask. You don't get scared and run. On my part, I will not try to surprise you with a party again."

"I promise to work on jumping to conclusions. And I won't run again. I trust you. I latched onto your words as an excuse because I was afraid. Falling in love is terrifying."

I raise an eyebrow. "Really? I didn't find it terrifying at all."

Hope lights his blue eyes. "Does this mean you love me?"

"Of course, I love you. I would have broken one of these plates over your head if I didn't."

"Speaking of plates…"

"Why? Why are we speaking of plates? Why aren't you ravishing me?"

He moans. "I want to. Trust me, I want nothing more in the world."

"But…"

"All of our friends should be showing up any minute now."

My brow furrows. "All of our friends?"

"Lucas, Flynn, and Hudson wanted me to do a grand gesture. I refused but they insisted on at least having a party."

"What about Caleb? Is he not in favor of grand gestures?"

"Nah. He was more in favor of kicking my ass."

I smile. "Remind me to thank him later."

"Troublemaker." He reaches for me but freezes. "Do I have permission to touch you?"

I jump into his arms. "Yes."

"Thank fuck," he mutters before his lips mold to mine. I sigh as his flavor hits me. I missed this. I missed him. I thought I lost it all. I've never been happier to be wrong. And I hate being wrong.

The door bangs open and I wrench my lips from Eli's.

"Awesome!" Chloe shouts. "They made up."

Sophia pushes her. "You know they made up. You were watching through the keyhole."

Eli chuckles. "Your friends are nuts."

"Our friends."

"Our friends," he repeats. "I love you, Lace."

"And I love you."

Chapter 33

"New rule. No promising to beat people up at a party." ~ Eli

Eli

Paisley steps away from me but I snatch her arm and bring her close. I'm not letting her get far away from me ever again. I can't breathe when I'm away from her.

Her friends approach with their partners. I smile at them. The women wave, but the men appear pissed.

"We need to steal her away for a moment." Sophia shackles Paisley's wrist and drags her away.

Flynn, Lucas, Hudson, and Caleb are wearing matching scowls. Paisley may have forgiven me but apparently, they haven't.

"Don't make us hijack your plane again," Caleb grumbles.

I sigh. "You didn't exactly hijack the plane."

He narrows his eyes. "But we could have."

Lucas groans. "Can you stop discussing crimes you plan to commit in front of me?"

"Why are you such a law abiding person?" Hudson asks.

"I'm a cop, remember?"

Hudson chuckles. "I can't believe Chloe married a cop."

Lucas waggles his eyebrows. "Trust me. Chloe enjoys me being a cop. Especially my handcuffs."

"Ew." Flynn feigns retching. "No. Chloe's a sister to me. I don't want to hear about whatever you get up to with her."

Lucas shrugs. "Your loss. I could teach you a lot about handcuffs in the bedroom."

Flynn smirks. "Dude, I don't need handcuffs to satisfy my woman."

Caleb groans. "I went to high school with your women. I don't need to hear this shit."

Lucas scratches his neck. "Didn't you go to high school with Maya?"

Hudson claps his back. "Congrats on the baby, man. Nova is beyond excited our children are going to grow up together."

I glance across the room and notice Paisley holding Iliana in her arms. The vision of her holding a little hazel-eyed baby with red hair hits me. I want that. I want her stomach swollen with my baby. I want to give her the family she never had growing up.

Flynn snaps his fingers in front of my face. "Earth to Eli."

"What?"

He grins. "If you had told me Sophia and her friends would all find love, I never would have believed you."

I glare at him. "What do you mean? There's nothing wrong with Paisley."

He shakes his finger. "Pretend all you want that Paisley's the normal one amongst the women but don't forget she's also the woman with the knowledge of chemistry." I must appear confused because he explains. "Chemistry they use in their pranks such as exploding stink bombs."

I shiver. At least the red dye didn't stink up my office.

Paisley pushes her way through the men to me. "I need your help."

Hudson waggles his eyebrows behind her back. "I bet she does," he mutters.

I push Paisley behind me before confronting him. "You will treat Paisley with the respect she deserves or I'll be the one breaking out the chemistry set. Understood?"

He smiles. "Just checking."

I roll my eyes. "Are you done with your brotherly approval shit now?"

He shrugs. "I am. But I don't speak for the rest of them."

Paisley tugs me away. "We'll speak to you later," she calls over her shoulder.

She stops in the hallway. "Chemistry set?"

"Forget it. What do you need my help for?"

She lifts the bag I didn't notice she was carrying. "Maya brought me an outfit to change into. Apparently, my jeans and t-shirt aren't appropriate clothing for a party."

I smirk. "And you need my help to change."

She slaps my shoulder. "No, silly. I thought you needed saving."

I step close and wrap my arms around her. "And you came to my rescue."

She rolls her eyes. "Of course, I did. I will always come to your rescue."

I kiss her nose. "And I'll always come to yours."

"I don't need a man to rescue me."

"Don't care. I'll rescue you anyway."

"I love you, Eli."

Those words hit me in my chest and spread warmth throughout my body. I will never tire of her telling me she loves me. I don't deserve her. Not after what I did. But I'm not letting her go. I will show her every single day for the rest of our lives that she made the right choice when she forgave me.

"And I love you, Lace."

I dip my head toward hers but she pushes me away. I scowl.

She points to the doorway where her friends are not even bothering to hide their eavesdropping. They wave and give us thumbs ups.

"Your friends are crazy."

"Our friends," she corrects. "And you should be used to crazy. I've met your brothers."

I groan. "And you encouraged them to be crazy."

She shrugs. "It's not my fault Miles thought he could eat ten funnel cakes without throwing up."

I snort. "You didn't encourage him?"

She widens her eyes and blinks. "He's a grown man. I don't know how I could ever influence his decision making."

I lift a brow.

She shrugs. "He needed to pay for all those times he called me Paisley the Perpetual Know It All."

"You've got everyone fooled."

She bats her eyelashes. "Fooled? I am who I am."

"You act like some nerdy girl who's in love with chemistry—"

"I do love chemistry. It's not an act."

I ignore her interruption. "But you're not some innocent. You're as devious as your friends."

"Why do you think we're such good friends?" She winks.

"People are arriving!" Sophia yells.

"You better make it a quickie," Chloe adds.

I wrap an arm around Paisley's shoulders and lead her away from the ballroom.

"Where are we going?" she asks when we pass the restrooms.

"To our room."

"Our room?"

"I didn't want to drive after the party, so I got us a suite."

"Suite," she mutters before narrowing her eyes on me. "And you assumed I'd stay in this suite with you."

"Hoped, Lace. Hoped. You can't blame a man for hoping."

"You're lucky I forgave you or I'd tell you what I think of a man hoping after breaking my heart."

My stomach clenches as guilt fills me. I never should have jumped to conclusions. And I should have at least let her explain. Why didn't I let her explain? Because I was a chicken shit.

I open the door to our suite and draw her inside. I set her bag on the couch before stalking toward her. She holds her ground.

My Lace doesn't shy away from anyone or anything. I couldn't admire her more.

I palm her neck. "I am more sorry for hurting you than I can ever express." I kiss her nose. "But you can't bring up how I hurt you every single time we have a fight or disagreement. It's no way to move forward together."

She sighs. "I know. I'm sorry. It's still raw."

"Which is why you're getting a pass today."

Her eyebrows raise. "I'm getting a pass today? What about tomorrow?"

"Tomorrow I'll spank your ass."

Her eyes flare but she purses her lips. "What if I don't want you spanking me?"

I massage her neck. "Don't lie, Lace. You want my hand on your naked ass. You want me to stare at the red imprint while I pound into you from behind. Preferably while you're bent over the sofa with your skirt around your waist."

Her breath hitches. "What if I'm not wearing a skirt?"

"All the better if you're naked. I can play with those pretty titties while I sink as deep inside of you as I can. I'll make you come as many times as I want."

"As you want?" She tries to sound sassy but she can't fool me. She's rubbing her thighs together to relieve the tension building there. My girl loves dirty talk.

I wind my arm around her waist and pull her near until her breasts push against my chest and she can feel how hard I am for her.

"Is there something you want, Lace?"

I begin tracing kisses along her jaw. She arches her back to give me better access to her neck and I draw a line with my tongue from her jaw down her neck to her shoulder where I nibble on her skin.

"W-w-we're supposed to be at the party."

I hide my grin at her stutter against her neck. "Why?"

"It's your birthday party. You can't miss it."

I shrug. "I've missed fourteen birthday parties. What's one more?"

She pushes me away. "You are not missing another birthday party. I won't allow it."

I chuckle. "You won't allow it?"

"Nope. You're not letting your dad rule your life anymore. Starting today."

"Who's going to enforce this rule?"

"I am. I'm not leaving you. I'm not running away. And you can't push me away. We're in this together."

Something settles in me at her words. Those are the words I needed to hear. I love you sounds fantastic coming from her but announcing we're in this together is what I need.

"If I agree, I want drunk sex with you tonight."

She sighs. "I guess I can agree to your terms."

I reach for her again – she didn't say we couldn't fool around a bit before the party – but her phone beeps with a message and she rushes for it.

Her eyes widen as she reads the text. "Chloe says your assistant and your brother are screaming at each other."

I groan. "I swear my brothers ruin everything."

"Come on." She nabs my hand. "Let's go find out what's wrong."

I allow her to lead me out of the hotel suite. I'll let her lead me wherever she wants to go. She wants to explore the nine circles of hell? I'll buy some fire-resistant hiking boots.

Paisley is my person. I fucked it up before but I know better now. I'm hanging on tight.

Chapter 34

"I didn't sign up for this." ~ Dakota

DAKOTA

I park my car in front of *The Hideaway Haven Resort* and whistle. This place is super fancy. A few years ago – before I started working for Eli, the billionaire owner of *Buccaneer's Whiskey* – I would have tucked tail and ran away. But now I'm used to fancy stuff.

Although, mostly it's answering the phone from other rich people, reserving suites in swanky hotels, arranging for Eli's private jet to pick him up – you know, totally normal rich person stuff.

I'm not usually invited to the parties. But today isn't strictly a rich person party. It's Eli's surprise birthday party.

I roll my eyes. Eli is such a man sometimes. He almost ended his relationship with the woman he loves because he overheard her planning a surprise for him. Dork.

I exit my vehicle and slam the door shut. I open the trunk where the present Eli's brothers bought for him is. I don't know what it is. All I know is it's a big ass box and it's heavy as shit.

I wrestle the box out of the trunk. But now I need to shut the trunk and I have zero hands available. I'm not about to set the box on the ground. There's no way I'll be able to lift it.

I lean against the car and use my chin to drag the trunk down. I bend my knees as the trunk slowly closes. It's almost latched when my foot slips causing my chin to move and I lose my hold on the trunk. It snaps open and whacks me in the face.

"Whiskey nuts. That hurt," I mutter as I blink my eyes.

"What the hell are you doing? Are you trying to hurt yourself?"

Rhett yanks the box from me. I wish I could say I fought him for control of the box but my upper body strength does not match his. Rhett's muscles have muscles. What I wouldn't do to touch his naked skin and discover how those muscles feel up close and personal.

Too bad the guy is a total control freak. And no one is controlling my life. Not anymore.

"I was trying to bring your brother's present into the party." I slam the trunk shut.

"What the hell did you buy him?" He narrows his eyes. "Why are you buying your boss expensive gifts? Do you have a crush on him? He's not available."

I hold up a hand. "Stop, Mr. High and Mighty. *I* didn't buy Eli a present." I did but it's a card with a gift certificate for a couples' massage and fits in my purse. "This is *your* present for Eli."

"This isn't my present. I would never ask a woman to bring a present."

My nostrils flare and I fist my hands at my hips. "Because a woman can't handle bringing a present? The Middle Ages are calling. They miss you and your misogynistic ass."

"I'm not misogynistic. I'm a gentleman."

I snort. "Do you even know what the definition of gentleman is?"

"It's a man who carries things for a woman and opens her door for her."

I open my mouth but I have no retort. His answer was actually kind of good.

"Whatever. Carry the present inside. I don't care. I was doing the Raider brothers a favor."

I start to stomp off but he hollers my name.

I whirl around. "What?"

He nods to the door. "Can you open the door for me?"

I jerk the door open with such force it nearly whacks me in my face. I have to hold the door with both hands to stop its vibrations.

Rhett smirks as he passes me. "The door came up and nearly bit you, did it?"

"You forgot to say thank you, Mr. Supposed Gentleman," I holler after him.

He flicks his hand. Is that supposed to be a thank you? I don't think so. And he can stop showing off how strong he is now. Holding the box with one arm. Why are jerks always the most sexiest men?

I follow Rhett into the ballroom and my jaw drops to the floor. Holy mermaids in the sea! This is awesome.

I don't know where to look first. There are old whiskey barrels and mini wooden crates filled with vintage-style rum bottles scattered around the room. The tables are decorated with shimmering tablecloths that mimic ocean waves. And the ceiling is lit up with a million twinkle lights.

"Pretty cool, isn't it?" Blossom says as she throws her arm over my shoulder.

"It's amazing." I scan the room. "Where's your boss?"

She waggles her eyebrows. "Probably the same place your boss is."

"I'm happy for Paisley and Eli but I hope I never walk in on them accidentally again." I shiver. "I do not need to see my boss's naked ass."

She scrunches her nose. "I don't know. I wouldn't mind seeing more of a certain Raider brother's ass."

"Jaxon is still avoiding you?"

She sighs. "Yep. He's not very stealth about it either. I walk into a room and he turns around and walks out. He actually walked into a wall once. He just stood there for a minute. I think he was pretending to be invisible."

I giggle. "I can't believe you managed to kiss him in the first place."

"I have magical powers." She winks.

Chloe skips toward us. "What are you two whispering about over here?"

I know better than to answer. Chloe is super nosy. I motion to the gift table. "We're guessing what's in the big box from Eli's brothers."

She rubs her hands together. "I hope it's a prank. I was forbidden from pulling a prank today." She pouts. "Nova and Maya are no fun."

I elbow her. "You're just mad two of your drinking buddies can't drink."

She grins. "But you're not pregnant or breastfeeding, are you?"

I open my mouth to answer but Rhett shouts before I can. "What the hell? You're pregnant?"

I shush him. "I'm not pregnant."

I can't even remember the last time I had sex. There is literally zero chance of me being pregnant. Unless vibrators suddenly carry sperm. In which case, I'm in big trouble.

"Why did Chloe say you are?"

"Can you keep your voice down?"

Those bright blue eyes he shares with his brothers narrow on me. I wish he was gazing at me intently because he was planning on devouring my mouth but Mr. High and Mighty would never lower himself to have a relationship with the hired help. Never mind he didn't grow up with money and he's basically hanging on the coattails of his brother.

"Answer the question," he grumbles.

I'll deny it to my dying day but his grumbling has nerve endings waking up all over my body. Damn him and his sexy voice. And his sexy eyes. And his sexy muscles.

"Have you met Chloe? She's a troublemaker down to her bones." I motion to her and Chloe widens her eyes. "See? Told you."

"Do I not appear innocent?" Chloe asks.

Blossom giggles next to her. "I've watched you threaten to gut a patron for not leaving a fifteen-percent tip. Innocent got up and walked away the second it saw you coming."

Chloe beams. "Thank you."

"It wasn't a compliment," Blossom mutters.

"I'm getting a drink," I declare and start to walk away. Rhett shackles my wrist to stop me. I raise an eyebrow at him. "Do you want to remove your hand from my body?"

He immediately lets go and raises his hands. "Answer my question."

"Ask an intelligent question and I'll consider it."

"Are you fucking pregnant?"

"No!" I shout. "Are you happy? The entire island will know I haven't had sex in over a year within the hour. Thanks for nothing."

I stomp away.

"You haven't had sex in a year?" he yells after me.

I do the mature thing. I give him the finger and keep walking.

If I wasn't his brother's assistant and work in the same building as him, I'd be glad to never see the controlling, domineering man again. Unfortunately, I have no choice.

The job with Eli offers benefits. And I need my benefits.

Chapter 35

SEVERAL MONTHS LATER

Eli

I freeze when I hear the door open. Shit. Paisley's home. I throw everything in the suitcase and shove it under the bed.

I sprint to the bathroom and flush the toilet. I'm washing my hands when she walks in.

"Hey, Lace. You're home early."

She narrows her eyes on me. "What are you doing here?"

I furrow my brow. "What do you mean? You gave me a key."

What an argument it took for her to give me that key. She used every stalling technique in the universe. *I'm not ready. It's too soon. We need to slow down.*

I was ready to move in together after she said she loved me at my birthday party. Paisley has other ideas about how fast our relationship should go. Which is why I'm hurrying things along on my own.

She crosses her arms over her chest. "You're not fooling me."

"Sorry, Lace. You're going to have to explain. I have no idea what you're talking about."

She lifts an eyebrow. "No idea? That's the excuse you're going for?"

I raise my hands. "What's up with you? I've been waiting for you in your house when you came home from work before."

"You know damn well your presence in my house is not why I'm annoyed."

Crap. She figured me out. I should have known I couldn't fool her. Paisley is the most intelligent and observant woman I know.

But I'm not giving in. I can be just as stubborn as she is.

"I do?" I scratch my chin.

She throws her arms in the air with a huff. "If you won't admit it, I'll show you the proof."

She spins around and marches to the bedroom. I trail after her. Of all the days for her to catch me.

Paisley scans her bedroom before getting to her knees and searching under the bed. I debate several excuses but it's no use. She knows exactly what's happening here.

She drags the suitcase out and sets it on the bed. "Do you want to explain?"

"Do I have to?"

"No. But an explanation would be nice."

I sigh. Time to lay my heart on the line. I sit on the bed and grasp her hands. I tug until she's forced to straddle me.

"I want you to live with me."

She purses her lips. "I'm well aware of this since you make an underhanded comment about us not living together at least twice a day."

"Twice a day?"

"Yesterday morning you remarked how it would be easier to drive together to work if we were living in the same house. And then, at lunch, you claimed if we were living together we could go home for a quickie."

My cock twitches. We didn't go home for a quickie. Instead, I trapped her in her office and took her against the wall. It was awesome. Every time with Paisley is awesome. Sex with her gets better and better every time. It's amazing.

"I'm not wrong."

She crosses her arms over her chest. "I've explained how I'm not ready to move in together."

I lay my palm on her cheek. "No, Lace. You've made excuses because you're scared."

Her eyes narrow. "I am not scared."

I lean close. "Prove it."

Her eyes spit daggers at me. "You are not going to dare me into moving together."

Damn. It was worth a try. It's worked before.

"But you are afraid."

She glances away. "Being concerned about jumping into a relationship too soon is not an indicator of fear."

I pinch her chin and force her gaze to meet mine. "Lace, love of my life, we are not jumping into a relationship. We've been tap dancing around each other for years. I know what my heart wants. And it wants you. Hell, if I knew you didn't approve of marriage, I would have already proposed."

"Instead, you're gradually moving all of my things into your house."

I shrug. "I have no remorse."

She snorts. "Of course, you don't."

"What do you expect? You can't possibly think I'm going to apologize for wanting the woman I love to live with me."

"It's a big step. I don't want to be dependent on you for housing."

I smirk. "I have a solution to your problem."

"If you dare me again, I'm going to deny you sex for a week."

I chuckle. "As if you can resist me for a week."

She sniffs and lifts her nose in the air. It's adorable. "I can and I will."

"Good thing I'm not going to dare you then."

I pull a manila envelope out of my pocket and hand it to her.

She doesn't accept it. "What's this?"

I wiggle it. "You won't find out unless you open it."

She snatches it from me and starts to stand. I grasp her hips to keep her right where she is. I want to be near when she reads the documents.

She frowns at me but doesn't put up a fight. Instead, she flicks open the envelope and removes the paperwork. She scans the first page and her frown deepens. She flips through the entire document without speaking a word.

A pit grows in my stomach. Is she going to reject my proposal? Reject me?

"Well?" I push when I can no longer handle the silence.

"This proves it." She shoves the document back into the envelope and throws it on the bed. "You're crazy."

"I'm crazy because I deeded you half of my house?"

She nods. "Yes."

"Why is it crazy to give the woman I plan to spend the rest of my life with half of the house I want her to make into our home?"

She throws her arms over my shoulders. "Because I would have moved in without ownership of the house."

"When would you have moved in? After our children graduate from college?"

"No. Next month."

My breath hitches. "Next month?"

"I have it all planned out. I didn't want to move in together until six months after your birthday party. In two weeks, it'll have been six months. Basically, you wasted a lot of money for nothing."

I growl. "Not for nothing. I want us to be equal partners. I want you to have half of my wealth."

She shakes her head. "I don't want your money."

"Too bad. You're getting it anyway."

She shrugs. "I'll just spend it on good causes."

"If you want to donate to good causes, we should probably attend a few more charity events."

My blood heats as I imagine her in the green dress she wore on our first date to the fundraiser in D.C. The memory of bending her over my couch and sliding into her warm heat has my cock hardening and lengthening. Sex with Paisley is always fantastic but that night was one of my favorites.

"Fine. But I'm not having sex in the jet."

I dig my hands into her hips and haul her near until her breasts press against my chest. "Lace, we are totally having sex in the jet. Probably more than once."

She sniffs. "The flight crew are literally feet away. No thanks."

"Feet away?" I lift an eyebrow. "Are you saying my jet is small?"

I lift my hips to press my cock against her core. Her eyes flare and she gasps.

"No," she sighs. "Your jet is not small."

I nibble her jaw. "Are you going to move in with me?"

"In two weeks."

I bite her earlobe and she moans. "Are you scared to move in with me earlier?"

"I'm not scared. I have a schedule."

I kiss the sensitive skin behind her ear and she tilts her neck to give me better access. "Prove it."

She scowls at me. "Stop daring me."

I lift her up and throw her on the bed before climbing on top of her. I shackle her wrists and lift her arms above her head.

"Paisley Bardot, do you love me?"

"Yes," she breathes out.

"Do you want to spend the rest of your life with me?"

"Yes."

"Are you going to give me children?"

I hold my breath. We haven't discussed having children yet.

"Yes."

Satisfaction winds through me. This woman is everything. And she's mine.

"Are you going to move in with me?"

Her eyes flash.

"Put me out of my misery, Lace. Agree to move in with me."

"Fine. But I'm keeping my house."

I figured as much. It'll make a good investment property.

I rip her jeans open. "This is going to be fast. The movers will be here in an hour."

"Wh—"

Her question is cut off when I shove two fingers into her pussy. Her warm, wet pussy.

"I love you, Lace. I will give you everything you want. Even if you don't know you want it. Or are afraid to want it."

She rears up and bites my jaw. "Prove it."

About the author

D.E. Haggerty is an American who has spent the majority of her adult life abroad. She has lived in Istanbul, various places throughout Germany, and currently finds herself in The Hague. She has been a military policewoman, a lawyer, a B&B owner/operator and now a writer.

Printed in Dunstable, United Kingdom

77741890R00163